THE FAERIE RACE BOOK ONE

THE SORCERY TRIAL

CLAIRE LUANA
J.A. ARMITAGE

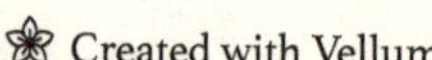

1
_____

I noticed two things in quick succession. One—the tips of his ears tapered to a delicate point. And two—his white button-down had been soaked in a tidal wave of coffee. The first meant he was a faerie. The second meant he had the misfortune of running into me.

My hands shook before me, empty of the carrying tray and the four venti quadruple shot Americanos I had just bought with the intention of ferrying them back to the studio headquarters. My pulse pounded like a jackhammer in my ears, adrenaline coursing through me.

The perky woman behind the counter goggled at us, adding to my unease.

I narrowed my eyes at her, hoping she would get the point that I didn't really need an audience right now. We were in Hollywood for goodness sakes—huge stars of the screen frequented this coffee shop day in, day out. Of course, if it was merely a famous actor I'd thrown coffee all over, my heart wouldn't be beating like a marching band, and none of this would be an issue. No, the male in front of me was no actor. He was a faerie. Here. In Los Angeles.

I took a deep breath and tried to keep my breakfast on the inside. Down on the floor, the four now-empty cups with my name misspelled on all of them—Jack instead of Jacq—mocked me, swimming as they were in a sea of black and pale brown liquid.

The faerie male was hissing in and out, his hands pulling his wet button-up away from his body, rivulets of steaming coffee running down his dark jeans onto wingtip shoes. "An oracle for a cousin, and I did not see that coming!" He barked a laugh, shaking off his shock. "If I wasn't awake before, I am now. I just expected to get my caffeine hit by drinking it."

"I'm sorry," I stammered, my thoughts racing almost too fast to catch. In the blink of an eye, I took him all in. His honey-gold locks falling over his forehead with a tousled elegance even a Disney prince would envy. Tan skin, tawny and glowing. Angled cheekbones, square jaw, and teeth as straight as a white-picket fence.

I had seen pictures of faeries every day for the last ten years. Since the existence of the fae and faerie realm had been exposed to all of humankind, they'd been news. Internet headlines, network stories, and viral videos. They were everywhere. And nowhere. Because faeries couldn't be in the mortal world, not without a visa from the ICCF, the International Coalition for Cooperation with Faeries. And mortals couldn't go into Faerwild.

I knew of their ethereal beauty in the way that you know a wildfire is hot. But that knowledge doesn't compare to standing next to the inferno and feeling it burn.

To be face to face with one in real life was terrifying. Exhilarating. No, definitely terrifying, I corrected myself.

"It was a most unfortunate accident," the faerie said. He looked young, maybe only a couple of years older than me.

Twenty? Twenty-one? But I knew that looks were deceptive when it came to those of a faerie persuasion. He could be a hundred. He could be a thousand. However old he was, he was at ease in his skin in a way that few mortals managed. Even drenched in coffee, he was relaxed, friendly. He didn't *seem* dangerous. And it was that fact that scared me most of all.

"It was," I managed. "It was my fault. I wasn't looking where I was going." It wasn't technically true. It'd been like a slow-motion movie crash. Once I had caught sight of him, once I had realized what he was...I'd been unable to avert disaster. I could see him there, but my mind refused to believe it. So I just kept walking.

"I'm more worried about the depth of your coffee addiction. Can a human even drink that much caffeine and live?"

I wrinkled my brow, silent for a moment before I realized he was teasing me. The murderous creatures could joke?

Years of resentment and pain bubbled under the surface, so close it made my skin itch. Yet, he seemed so normal. If it wasn't for those ears of his and that weird aura of confidence that so few could pull off...I wouldn't have even known he was a faerie in the first place.

"They weren't for me. I work at the studio," I managed, nodding my head in the direction of the headquarters, where right now my high-strung bosses were, no doubt, wondering what was taking me so long to deliver their next caffeine hit. They were not the kind of people that liked to wait, and as I was the lowest monkey on the Hollywood ladder, I was extremely expendable. A fact that I was reminded of on a daily basis.

"Cool. What do you do?" he asked, shoving his hands in

his pockets, seeming to have forgotten the aromatic liquid still dripping down him.

"I'm a gopher."

He cocked his head. "You're not like any gopher I've ever seen. I'd be very impressed to see a human turn into a small woodland creature. Not even most faeries could pull that off."

I ran my fingers through my blonde ponytail, a nervous gesture from childhood. "Is that another joke?"

The faerie chuckled. "If you have to ask, it means it wasn't a very good one."

"Not gopher. Go-fer. Like, go get stuff. I do random odd jobs. Coffee, errands, whatever punishment my boss can dream up for me. It's just for now." Everyone in the industry knew what a gopher was. The fact that he had to ask marked him as even more of an outsider.

"I want to do stunts," I blurted out. As soon as the words left my mouth, I wanted to swallow them. Why was I even telling him that? It wasn't as though I was embarrassed by my job. Plenty of stars started their Hollywood careers in much the same way.

"You're going to be a stunt woman?" His green eyes widened and crinkled up at the edges. He seemed genuinely impressed. I guess there wasn't much call for stunt people in Faerwild. "What kind of stunts do you do?"

I weighed the question, wondering if he was genuinely interested or if his question disguised some sinister intent. It was so hard to tell. I decided that it didn't really matter if I told him. It was hardly a state secret.

"Whatever they want. I can drive, I can ride horses, I can fight. I'll do it all." I managed, though I still couldn't believe his curiosity was genuine. To a faerie, I was as important as a woodland creature. As an insect. That's how faeries saw us mere mortals. Something to play with. And to squash when they got bored.

"Sounds like you're attracted to danger." A mischievous smile played across his handsome face, and warning bells rang in my mind. That's what I expected. That's what I needed to watch out for. That's what got Cass.

"I should go," I said. "I need to place another order and get back to work. I'm really sorry about your clothes." I wasn't *that* sorry. His clothes looked expensive—perfectly tailored to fit his lean, muscled form. He probably had a leprechaun slave or something who could make him another set.

"Don't worry about it," he said. "In fact, I can fix it right up."

His hands were out of his pockets before I could protest, moving in an unnatural motion. My heart seized in my chest as his lips moved, mouthing strange nonsense syllables. He was doing magic.

Every fiber within me told me to run, to flee from him, and not look back. But I was rooted to the spot, fascinated and horrified in turn. I hadn't been around magic for two years—not since Cassandra and her coven were playing around in the attic with candles and runes. Since she started sneaking out to meet some guy, a guy who happened to have glowing golden eyes and pointed ears. Since she disappeared into the field behind our ranch with him and never came back.

At the thought of my older sister, my heart squeezed in my chest like a vice. Even as the coffee cups and carrying tray were floating back into the air, the dark coffee pooling and flowing back into them like real-life CGI, I thought of her. I held her in my mind, reminding me. Why, no matter how beautiful they appeared, or enchanting they seemed, I hated them. All of them.

The girl behind the counter was full on staring now, which somehow irked me even more. It was a detail to focus on. A safe, human detail.

The blond faerie seemed ridiculously pleased with himself as he took the tray of full Americanos and handed it back to me. "You're welcome," he said with a wink.

I pushed past him, even the words *thank you* sticking in my throat.

I hurried back through the lot, past the parked golf carts and a gaggle of extras clad in Viking attire. It wasn't until I passed into the glass door of the headquarters that I realized I hadn't even thought to ask the faerie, why was he here?

2

My mind was still whirring as I passed through security and headed up to the conference room. My boss, John Ashton, wasn't a Hollywood bigwig, but he was getting there. He ruled his little corner of the studio with an iron fist, and everyone knew he was just biding his time until he hit the big time—until he found *the one*. "The one" was a mythical TV show that would become an instant sensation the world over, skyrocketing John to fame and fortune in the process.

It's not that his shows had all been flops—a few, like *Down Under* (a reality show set in Australia) and *Psychic Pirates* (about, well, psychic pirates)—were several seasons in. But none had catapulted John to the big league where he thought he deserved to be.

I expected the usual combination of condescension and cursing as I entered the conference room, my coffee run having taken much longer than normal, thanks to my run-in with the faerie. I had a lie ready on my lips—but John threw me completely by thanking me and asking me to put the coffee on a table in the corner. His handsome face was tense with barely-veiled excitement.

I did as he asked, making sure to empty my pockets of the little pink packets of sweetener he liked, plus some packets of sugar in case his guests turned out to be the only people in Hollywood not on a diet. There were three other people in the glass conference room, two handsome men in Armani suits and a sleek-looking woman in ridiculously high Louboutin heels. It wasn't difficult to figure out that these three were the big guns John always talked about. I was just about to leave when I heard the word "fae."

My ears pricked. It couldn't be a coincidence. I'd seen a faerie up close for the first time in my life, and suddenly, my boss and his guests were talking about them?

"How many are we gonna send in?" one of the men asked, his voice gruff.

John replied. "I haven't worked out all the details yet. The king hasn't been very specific, but I'm thinking we do it in teams. One boy and one girl maybe. One human, one faerie."

I swallowed the lump that had formed in my throat, barely able to breathe. If he was talking about a king, it could only mean one thing. They were talking about the Faerie King. They were sending people over the Hedge. Into Faerwild. The faerie realm. Faerwild only ever conjured up one thought in my mind, and it was the same thing I'd been thinking about ever since my run-in at the coffee shop. My sister, Cass. It was like she and the entirety of Faerwild were linked in my mind. It was impossible to think about one without the other creeping in.

Maybe...it was a borderline obsession. One that I'd kept to myself for a long time, one that had nearly taken over my life before I'd purposely decided to move on with my life and distance myself from it. Literally as well as figuratively. A year ago, the minute I graduated high school, I'd left my easygoing hometown and my parents to try my luck in Hollywood. I knew no one and had nothing to my name but my old Toyota Corolla, the desire to get away from my past, and the thirst to make it as a stuntwoman. Unfortunately, the past had caught up with me this very morning, and I'd thrown coffee all over it. Not that I thought the handsome faerie was the one that took Cass, but he was close enough.

I'd had to at least *try* to give up my obsession with finding Cass. For my chances of finding her were nil—if the ICCF couldn't, what hope did I have? Humans weren't allowed in Faerie at all. Not until very recently anyway, and I'd heard that even with a good reason, it took months to get through the paperwork and red tape necessary to get a decree from the king.

I'd tried; of course, I had. As soon as they'd opened the portals to humans a few months ago, I'd turned up at a faerie circle begging to be let in. The ICCF goons guarding the portal had laughed at me. As a gopher at a TV studio—a lowly human—I had no chance. I couldn't give them a credible reason. Telling them that I thought a faerie had kidnapped my sister was hardly going to get me through.

"I like the idea, John," the gruff man spoke again. "This thing could be huge. But I need you to nail down the specifics."

"Could be? It'll be the TV show of the year...of the century! Almost no human has ever ventured over the Hedge before, and certainly, no camera crews have ever been allowed in. Can you imagine how many people will watch the show? Even if they don't like the idea of a race, they'll tune in just to see what it's like over there."

"I want to know," piped in the woman.

"Fine," gruff man agreed. "We'll greenlight the show. I like the premise. I love the danger aspect. But I want you on this quickly. As you said, this is going to work because no one has been there before. If those show-stealing idiots over at NBC get there first, this whole venture will be pointless."

I stood silently, hoping none of them realized they still hadn't gotten their coffee yet. I was afraid to turn around. At the moment, I was practically invisible to them, but if I drew any attention to myself, I might be thrown out before I heard the rest.

"I'm on it," John said. I could hear the excitement in his voice. It was a nice change from the hurried anger he usually spoke with.

"Don't let me down," the gruff man replied. I heard the squeak of his chair as he stood, followed by the squeaks of the other chairs. "I want all those details worked out and on my desk before my morning green juice on Monday."

"Monday?" John replied, his voice rising a notch. "That's three days away!"

"Is there a problem? If there is, I can get someone else on it."

John replied hastily. "No, no problem. The crown prince is in town to discuss it. I'm sure we can work out all the details."

"Good," barked the gruff man.

I turned to see the three execs leaving. John caught my eye, leaning back in his chair with a whoosh of exhaled breath.

"Bring my coffee over to me, would you? Oh and grab me one of those donuts too."

I arched a brow. Despite minimal body fat and near-perfect physique, John was always on some sort of paleo-Atkins-keto-whateverthelatestfad diet. I'd never seen a donut pass his lips once in the year I'd worked here. I'd come to the conclusion the man ran on coffee and air.

I picked up the biggest donut and his coffee and put them on the table before him.

He had a satisfied smile on his face, and that rattled me too. I was used to snarls and grimaces. This version of John was almost as foreign to me as the gorgeous faerie male had been.

Curiosity was burning me up, and I was just about to ask him about the show when he spoke first. "It's the one. The big break I've been telling you about! Today, we celebrate." He tore into his donut with a vengeance, coating his lips with sugar. He handed me back the coffee and pointed to the sweetener packet I'd laid on the table.

Getting the message, I ripped the package open and emptied the contents into his coffee, swirling it all around until the little white flecks dissolved.

"What's the show?" I asked innocently as if I'd not just spent the last five minutes eavesdropping on his conversation. "Something to do with the fae? Are you sending people into Faerwild?"

John nodded, his eyes closed in rapture as he chewed the donut. He swallowed, grabbing his coffee. "That's the plan. The Faerie King wants to bring people in to show us humans what it's really like. Something about furthering human-faerie relations or some such bullshit. I don't care why, only that I'm the one who will be producing the damn thing."

John gave a self-satisfied smirk and took a sip of his coffee. He nodded slightly to let me know that I'd done a good job with it. Much better than the time he threw his coffee at me for it being too cold.

"It's going to be a race. But better than a race. We'll have faerie-human teams, so there'll be plenty of drama. They'll have to dodge obstacles in rough terrain, avoid freakish faerie beasts, solve riddles. And, now that magic's out in the open and legal, we'll have that too. Magic—actual magic."

His eyes misted over as he held his hands out wide, complete with half-eaten donut. "Danger! Intrigue! Magic! Maybe even romance. God, this thing is going to be a gold mine! People are going to go nuts."

"Who are the contestants going to be?" I asked casually, trying to keep from sounding like I was too interested. If people were going over the Hedge, I was going to do everything in my power to be one of them.

"I don't know yet." He looked right at me, his chiseled jaw working. "I guess we'll do what all those talent shows do and hold auditions?" His blue eyes lit up. "That's it. We'll hold auditions. Great idea. Write it down."

It hadn't been my idea, and I wasn't his secretary, but I wasn't about to point either of those things out to him. Instead, I grabbed a pen and a notepad from the credenza against the wall and began to write.

"Anything else?" I asked once I'd finished writing the word 'audition' in black ink.

"Not yet," John barked, snatching the notepad out of my hand and reading that one word. He nodded thoughtfully at it.

Auditions. If they were holding auditions, that meant they weren't going to hire actors. They were looking for real people. My heart began to beat quicker once again. It was really getting a workout today what with everything going on.

"What will the auditions consist of?" I asked. If I was the first to know, maybe I could take advantage of my head start.

"Something really cool..." John answered, staring off

into space. I wondered what exactly he was picturing. "And dangerous."

"Something cool and dangerous?" I echoed back to him, trying to pluck up the courage to ask him the question I really wanted to ask. Cool and dangerous was so vague. It could mean anything. But did it matter? For a chance to find my sister, I'd skydive over shark-infested waters.

"Hmmm." John ran a hand through his perfect blond hair.

I plunged ahead. "Is there any chance I would be allowed to audition?" I asked, trying to keep my voice steady and my tone even.

When he turned to look at me, it was like he'd only just noticed I was in the room—even though we'd been conversing for the past few minutes.

John looked me up and down, and I tried to interpret what he saw. Pretty-enough blonde girl with hazel eyes? Not too tall, biceps slightly too big, boobs slightly too small? Jeans and boots scuffed from real labor, rather than bought that way at some overpriced boutique?

I stifled a sigh. It was plain to see from the expression on his face that despite me bringing him coffee twice a day for nearly a year, he didn't have the first clue who I was. And he wasn't impressed by what he saw.

"No," John answered abruptly, and just like that, my dream of finding my sister was shattered once again.

3

———

The auditions for *The Fantastic Faerie Race*, as the show was to be called, came together crazy fast, as everyone was worried that another network would find out and try to hijack the show. The entire lot was buzzing with the news; everywhere I went the word "faerie" was on someone's lips. I scowled each time I heard it, sinking deeper into my funk the closer we got to auditions.

I didn't really blame John for rejecting my request. I knew how it worked. They were looking for contestants who would make the best TV—the most beautiful or talented, the most drama-prone and self-destructive. There was a formula to putting together a reality show cast, and it seemed that aspiring stunt girls from Montana were not considered a key ingredient.

I buried myself in my tasks at work, keeping my head down, and in the evening, after sitting in the hour and a half of traffic it took to get home to my barely-affordable apartment in Irvine, I doubled my workouts. I went to my regular evening boot camp or MMA class and then went for a long run afterwards, trying to fit in some stairs or other resistance training. The physical exhaustion kept my mind from spinning too badly, thinking about Cass and how badly I was failing in my sworn promise to find her and bring her home.

The police and the ICCF had given up searching, my parents had lost hope, and after a year of her being gone, I'd given up too. Not hope, I never gave up hope, but I'd given up searching. What was the point when I knew in my heart where she was but couldn't get there. I'd trampled the fields and forests for miles around our home, hoping to find some portal they'd used, but even as I drove myself to exhaustion, I knew it was pointless. She was gone.

She'd been acting differently in the few weeks before she left. Distant. Secretive. Worried. Pulling away from me. So when Cass looked me in the eyes and begged me not to tell anyone she was going to be gone for a little while, it had been an easy promise to keep. I was just glad she was trusting me with something. But I was such an idiot—because I hadn't seen her shaking hands, the way her eyes darted about, for what they were. Signs I should have picked up on. Signs that everything was not okay—and that Cass was in trouble. I don't know what that faerie had on her, or how he forced her to leave, but she never would have left us by choice. Not Cass.

A year after she left, I finally admitted defeat and moved away from the bad memories, leaving my mother and father to grieve for another lost daughter. They knew where I was, and I called them all the time, but the guilt at leaving them still gnawed at my heart as it did when I thought of Cass and how I just let her walk out of all our lives.

Despite doing everything in my power to avoid all thought and mention of faeries, when the first day of auditions arrived, I found myself gravitating towards the far corner of the lot with everyone else. They'd been interviewing contestant candidates the past few days, and only the top contenders would have a chance to compete in the main auditions.

My eyes widened as I ducked into the cavernous space where the auditions were being held. In the span of a week, they had set up one of the most elaborate obstacle courses that I'd ever seen. Even knowing what miracle-workers Hollywood set-designers could be, it was impressive.

It was designed like a forest landscape—filled with gnarled trees and rough terrain, including a waterfall and craggy cliff face. I spotted a barbed wire fence, rope ladder, and—I held up a hand to shield my eyes as a gush of flame shot skyward—some sort of pyrotechnic geyser?

A group of people were talking on the edge of the course, and my feet moved inadvertently, pulling me closer. These must be the contestants. There were the types you would expect—tanned bodybuilders in tank tops and perky, tiny-waisted girls in sports bras and tight athletic shorts. But then there were others—strange forms and faces I'd never seen before. An incredibly tall pale man with white hair down to his waist, a lithe woman with green-tinged skin and curls of ivy in her emerald curls, a huge craggy creature that looked part mountain—could he be a giant? My mouth went dry at the sight of them. What kind of world contained creatures like these? And could my sister have survived it?

"Jacqueline?" a hesitant voice asked, and I turned to see a guy hurrying up to me, a friendly, partly apologetic smile on his face. He looked familiar... I struggled to place him.

"It is Jacqueline, right?" he asked.

"Uh, yeah. I go by Jacq," I said.

"Jacq." He grinned. He was cute, in a slightly doughy way, with brown curly hair and a bright smile. "Ben." He held out his hand, and I shook it. "We met at Christine's party a few months ago."

"Right." I sighed in relief at placing him. He'd been one of the many faces at my roommate Christine's housewarming party. She was an aspiring actress and was constantly hosting soirees to try to make connections. I usually tried to make myself scarce as I found her friends and her friends' friends to be fairly obnoxious human beings, but I'd stayed around for that one. "Ben. You're a... camera guy, right?"

"Yep!" he said proudly.

"Are you going to be working on FFR?" I asked, using the moniker that had quickly been attached to the new show.

"Yes!" His brown eyes lit up with excitement. "Each of the six teams is going in with one cameraman. It's going to be amazing. There's talk that we'll each have our own like... enchanted flying horse, or dragon, or something to ride above or alongside our team, out of danger, filming whatever happens. It's going to be epic."

"Sounds really cool." I smiled at him, marveling at how easy it was to mention dragons these days without batting an eye. Even in Hollyweird, the mention of real dragons would have sent someone to the loony bin just a few short years ago. Now, they were as passé as cats and dogs. What a strange world.

Ben grinned. "I'm the youngest cameraman to be selected," Ben said proudly. He did look young. Not much older than me in fact. But his enthusiasm was infectious.

"I thought electronics shorted out around faerie magic?" I asked. "How are you going to film it?"

"I guess the King has some sort of charm he'll give us to protect the electronics from the magical interference. It's going to be amazing." Ben was practically jumping up and down with excitement, and for a second, I was jealous. I wasn't sure I'd ever been as excited about anything in my life as he seemed to be right now.

I glanced over at the action happening on the set. There was one director in charge of it all, but a group of assistants with radios attached to their belts were working as contestant wranglers, busily shouting orders and trying to get everyone under control. To the untrained eye, it looked like a hot mess, but I was sure they knew what they were doing.

"What do you think of the teams?" I asked Ben. "Do you know who you want to be paired with?"

"Too soon to tell," Ben replied as we watched one of the faerie auditioners dart into the course ahead of schedule and a studio assistant in heels follow her, shouting after her.

"I think the dryad's kinda cute though." He blushed. How could he be attracted to these otherworldly creatures? There was something so alien about all of them, even those who did look human. The air crackled around them like some kind of magical aura, and though it was barely noticeable, I could feel it, even from this distance. It was like the whole atmosphere was sucked dry around them.

"Is she the green one?" I asked, though it didn't matter. I didn't know what a dryad was in the first place. I hadn't felt the need to major in mythical creatures in high school. It wasn't a topic I thought I'd need later on in life. I really should go to the library now that it turned out most of them weren't mythical after all, just living in a different plane of existence.

Ben nodded. "They say the Faerie King's heir is an obvious competitor. He'll get in no matter what. Nepotism at its finest, but what can you do?"

"Which one is he?" I asked, curiosity overcoming me. I searched the strange, handsome faces and started when I realized I recognized one of them. The golden-haired faerie from the coffee shop.

"He's that one," Ben nodded his head, lowering his voice. "Tristam Obanstone. Even his name sounds fancy."

"The handsome blond one?" My voice was faint, my ears burning. *Please, please tell me I did not spill four venti Americanos on the crown prince of Faerwild…*

"Yep, that's him."

"Of course, it is." I closed my eyes briefly, fighting my mortification.

"Oh, there's Katarina Ruskikov." Ben continued. "She's a Russian Olympic gymnast."

I eyed the blonde girl Ben was pointing out. She was tiny but totally ripped. "She came from Russia? For this?"

"Yep, it's drawn competitors from all over the world. Hmm, I don't envy her partner. He looks like he got up on the wrong side of the bed."

A tall, ebony-haired faerie male loomed over the Russian gymnast like a dark cloud. He wore all black—black jeans, black boots, and a black leather jacket. It was an understatement to say he looked out of place next to the neon spandex and tech-fabrics of the other competitors. Dark stubble shadowed the lines of his preternaturally handsome face. He looked like the angel of death, and with a face like that, some might go willingly to the grave.

As if he could hear my thoughts, his head swiveled in my direction, his piercing gaze locking on me. My breath caught in my throat. His coal-black eyes were lined with dark lashes so long they hardly looked natural.

"Jacq!" A figure moved into my line of sight, breaking me free from the prison of that faerie's eyes.

I pulled in a ragged breath. "John." I straightened. I'd never been so relieved to see my asshole boss.

He waved a paper at me. "I've got lunch orders for the contestants. We're filming all day, so I'm going to need you here until we wrap." He shoved the paper into my hands and spun on the heel of his expensive wingtip shoe, heading back towards the course.

"Duty calls," I told Ben.

Ben smiled at me. "Good to see you again, Jacq."

"You too." And I found I meant it. It was comforting to see a friendly face amongst the weirdness of this day.

JOHN WASN'T KIDDING. The auditions lasted *all* day and well into the night. The obstacle course was only the first part of the audition. There was also a magic test and some sort of logic exam. Apparently, there would be three legs of FFR, testing the contestants in those three areas. Physical prowess, magic, and intelligence.

It was well after midnight when John finally waved me off. I got to my car, a sad little teal Toyota Corolla, only to realize I had left my purse on the set after delivering a particularly large order of sandwiches. I swore, jogging back towards the building.

It was a nice night, warm and cloudless. You couldn't see many stars here, not with all the city lights, but a few peeked out at me. I felt a pang of homesickness. The stars back home were epic. They didn't call it Big Sky Country for nothing. Cass and I used to love pulling our sleeping bags out into the backyard and falling asleep under the glittering spray of the Milky Way. I wondered what the stars looked like wherever she was. Were the stars different over the Hedge?

The lights were low in the building, and the trees of the

obstacle course cast spindly shadows on the concrete. I found my purse tucked under the table where I'd left it, and pulled the long strap over my head. But as I turned to go, I paused. The obstacle course called to me, a forbidden siren song. I looked around. The building was empty and the cloying magic that had been suffocating me all day had now dispersed leaving only fresh air, or at least as fresh as the air of L.A. ever got. And I hadn't gotten my workout in tonight. It couldn't hurt to have one go, could it?

I'd spent all day watching the contestants running it. Some, such as the Russian gymnast had moved over it with such ease that they might as well have been merely crossing the road, but most had struggled. Some had barely stepped foot on it before falling at the first hurdle. Watching them all had left me itching to try it out. I hadn't been busting my butt in the gym for the last two years for nothing. I knew I could do it.

I strode quickly to the start of the course, dropping my purse at my feet and making sure I really was alone on the lot. I pulled off my flannel shirt, leaving only my white tank top. I examined my route as I pulled my hair into a tight ponytail.

And then I ran. Through the trees I dashed, dodging dark pine needles and hurdling over downed logs. I aimed for the post of the barbed wire fence, using it to launch myself over the prickly wire in one jump. A smile stretched onto my face, and I found myself laughing with the thrill of it. This is why I wanted to be a stunt girl. I never felt more like myself than when I had the wind in my hair and adrenaline coursing through my veins. Everything else fell away —my worries, my doubt, my failures. There was only the thrill. I was born for this.

Up I went, scaling the rope ladder, taking two or three

rungs at a time and jumping up onto the cliff face. The exploding fire geysers were turned off, but I was confident I could have dodged those, no problem. My legs and my lungs burned with effort as I sprinted the last leg, hurdling a makeshift river to dash the last few yards to the finish bell. I rang it proudly. I had kicked that course's ass just as I'd known I would.

The peal of the bell echoed loudly in the cavernous space, mingling with the ragged tempo of my breathing. The hairs on the back of my neck rose, and I stilled, looking around the shadowed building. I was overcome with the feeling that I was being watched.

"Hello?" I called, squinting my eyes, trying to see into the dark recesses and corners. The last echo of the bell died away, and I blew out a deep breath. I hurried down the stairs from the upper platform I'd summited and grabbed my shirt and purse, jogging towards the door. All the while, feeling certain that I wasn't alone.

4
____

"Have you seen this?" John thrust a newspaper under my nose as soon as I opened his office door. I took the paper from him and placed his coffee on the only part of his desk that wasn't covered in newsprint.

"That's only one, but it's everywhere. Look! This one has it on the front page!"

I glanced down at the paper in my hand. As John had said, it did indeed have FFR on the cover. Not that I was surprised. The race was a huge deal. I'd seen it mentioned everywhere. Even the comedians on the late night talk shows were making jokes about it.

"My secretary fielded three hundred calls yesterday from papers, magazines, and blogs asking if we would set up interviews with the faerie contestants. Thank all that's holy that we have them on contract right?"

"Right," I agreed, laying the paper atop the others. John wasn't the only one filled with excitement with all that was going on. I'd seen quite a number of the higher studio execs walking around with unusually wide smiles on their faces—

as if they were thinking about the even bigger bulges in their wallets. The FFR was an overnight sensation, and the show hadn't even started yet.

What it meant for me was that I was getting a lot of overtime, and John finally remembered my name.

Though I constantly tried to remind myself of what dangerous, duplicitous creatures faeries were, part of me couldn't help but be as excited as everyone else. Being on the lot meant I saw the action in real time and it was hard not to get sucked in. Like everyone else, I'd cheered when one of the underdogs got through and booed when the media's favorite was caught cheating. After two weeks of auditions, we were finally filming the last one before the actual race began.

Today, the top contenders would be competing against each other to score one of the coveted twelve spots in the race. Six humans and six faeries would be selected. Not only was a ton of money on the line (first place had a $2 million purse), but the Faerie King had announced that the winners would each be able to request a magical boon from him—a request or wish that he wouldn't be able to deny. It was like scoring one wish from the genie in Aladdin's lamp—that boon was more precious than gold. I tried not to think of how I could help Cass with that boon. The king would only have to snap his fingers, and I'd have my sister back. I stifled a sigh. It didn't matter. I wasn't allowed to compete.

For the final audition competition, the FFR execs had decided they needed something epic. So, they'd set up a two-mile-long loop course through the trails of the Topanga State Park.

Almost everyone in the studio had come out to watch—from the head of the studio himself to the kids that worked in the mailroom. The studio was milking the hype for all it was worth, so this last audition was being shown live to every country around the world. Whatever happened in the next twenty minutes would change the fate of these contestant's lives forever. Even those that lost would be set for life thanks to lucrative sponsorships.

No one wanted to lose though. I could see that money or magic wasn't the object of this for a lot of them. Every single contestant out there was looking to win a place. To prove to the world—mortal and faerie—that they were worthy.

The competitors' eyes gleamed as they lined up to start. They had no idea what awaited them in the hot, dusty two miles to come. I'd seen some of the obstacles and traps that had been set up, and I didn't envy them. This new course wasn't messing around.

I held my breath as the loud buzzer signaled the start of the audition. For purposes of the audition, every competitor was on their own. In the real race, there would be teams of two, but today, it was every human and faerie for him or herself.

As I watched, two competitors got tangled at the first hurdle, a trap net that had been laid over a hole in the ground. The huge giant became snagged in the net, and flailed out a huge hand, knocking the tiny Russian girl about ten feet. The girl had tears in her eyes as she tried to push to her feet, but I could see she'd been injured somehow by the fall.

"Looks like beauty and the beast is out," murmured John in my ear gleefully as the girl let out a long list of words in Russian which, if I had to guess, were extremely rude expletives. The giant answered her by giving her the finger.

"Oops," chuckled John in a most unprofessional manner. "The censors won't be happy about that."

Not that he cared. That would be talked about for weeks

to come, and he knew it. "No publicity is bad publicity," he added.

"And no cliché is a bad cliché, right, sir?" I replied, trying not to grin.

"Right, Jacq," he answered, proving he wasn't really listening to me.

I'd not actually seen the full course, so I decided to get away from the crowd. I could stay behind and watch the action on the huge screen that had been put up in the parking lot for the staff to watch, but on the screen, you couldn't smell the smoke from the pyrotechnics or feel the heat as the fire geysers went off.

There were several little trails running parallel to the course, shortcuts snaking across the dry terrain to other parts of the route. Apart from the unfortunate pair near the start, the other competitors would be well into the race by now, meaning I'd be left in peace to see what the designers had come up with and then watch the contestants as they came around.

Though I ached to run the course myself, it was almost as good to walk alongside it and see the obstacles up close. I jogged down the little trail to the other side, inhaling the hot scent of sagebrush and chaparral trees. I came out into the sunshine at the end of the trail, halting at the six-foot chain-link fence that separated me from the course.

A mad thought entered my mind. All I'd have to do was hop that fence, and I'd be on the course. I could tackle a few obstacles...maybe even make it to the finish. For a brief second, I considered it. All attention was on the competitors farther down the course—maybe no one would see me. It would be so easy...But if I did get caught, I'd probably get fired, and my dreams of someday being a stuntwoman would be over. I sighed and contented myself with jogging along the trail, using my imagination.

Unfortunately, before I was halfway round, my imagination began to play tricks on me. I heard the heavy breathing of someone who sounded like they were in pain. The part of the track I was at was heavily wooded, and so it was impossible to see exactly what it was making the sound.

I listened again and heard a cry of pain. Was it a sound effect or was someone really hurt? I stepped forward, deciding it was one of the many effects designed to disorient the contestants when I heard a voice. A female voice, coming from inside the track.

"Please, help me," the girl cried out.

The plea was answered by a male voice. "You got yourself into it; you're on your own getting yourself out."

"I can't," a woman's pained voice hissed between sobs.

"The studio staff will come to pick you up," the male's voice was deep and smooth as silk. The speaker was fae. I could feel it.

I listened a moment longer, but all I could hear was the woman's quiet sobs.

Frantic, I looked around me for help, but I was completely alone.

Getting over the fence was easy. Stopping my own heart from racing, knowing I was breaking the rules, not so much, but what else could I do? I couldn't leave her there. There were a number of paramedics and ambulances at the end of the track, but nothing in the middle.

"This would have been solved if I'd just been given a radio," I grumbled to myself as I dug my fingers into the links of the fence, launching myself skyward.

I dropped onto the dirt of the track in a lithe motion. From inside the track, the outside world no longer existed. The Los Angeles foothills disappeared as I plunged into a dense jungle. Just three steps in and I could have been in the depths of the Brazilian rainforest. The set designers had worked a miracle, adding towering trees and lush foliage. Sound effects of birds and wildlife filtered through the trees and the heat I'd felt on the other side of the fence was now blistering. I couldn't believe the state had allowed this! The politicians in Sacramento must be as caught up in FFR fever as the rest of the world.

The sound of the contestant's sobs led me to a small clearing with a body of water to one side. The girl—a staggering beauty with long golden hair—had gotten snagged in a trap. She was one of the human contestants. I didn't need to look for the telltale pointed ears of the fae to know she didn't have them. She didn't have the aura—the weird feeling about her that the faeries did. Apart from her Hollywood beauty, she was normal and scared. I looked at the trap her leg was caught in. Unlike the rope trap that had felled the giant, this one was metal with jagged teeth that had bitten into the flesh just above the ankle. Holy hell. Anger flared in me. I knew the studio wanted the danger to feel real, but this was crazy! All for a TV show?

If that wasn't bad enough, a huge crocodile was moving towards her with sinuous grace, its beady eyes focused on its next meal. At least that was fake, unlike the bear trap.

The girl started as I ran out from the bushes, dropping to my knees at her side.

"It's okay," I said. "The crocodile's animatronic. It won't hurt you." I pulled at the trap carefully as she winced in pain.

"I...I..." She looked at me through glassy eyes and took a deep breath. "I don't think it's animatronic."

I swiveled towards the crocodile, scrutinizing it. It *had* to be a fake. There was no way they'd put a live crocodile in here. They'd be sued for millions if anyone was too badly hurt...wouldn't they? I looked at the girl's leg. They hadn't seemed too concerned about putting this trap in here....

The crocodile snapped its sharp teeth together and whipped its tail. It took another step closer. It looked...really real. I knew animatronics were good these days...but...

"Oh my god," I whispered. A wave of cold washed over me, sending a sheen of sweat prickling over my skin. "It's real."

"That's what I just said!" the girl cried, trying to scooch away. She hissed as her movement pulled at the trap.

"Stay still," I commanded, wrenching at the jaws of the trap. If I didn't get her free of the trap soon, we'd both be crocodile lunch.

Using every ounce of strength I had, I managed to pull the jagged metal teeth from the girl's flesh long enough for her to pull her foot out.

"Come on, quickly!" I hauled the girl up on her good leg.

"I can't!" she cried, sagging against me.

I looked down to her injured leg and grimaced. It was a bloody mess. I'd have to haul her over my shoulder and carry her away from the crocodile.

"Hold on," I said as I pulled her weight over me, staggering for a moment before I caught myself. I'd squatted heavier weight than her before, but that hardly compared to trying to haul a teetering, crying person!

I made it past the crocodile and back to the fence.

"Help!" I cried, but there was nothing in sight but vegetation.

"I'm going to have to carry you over the fence," I stammered, wondering how exactly I was going to accomplish such a task. Getting over alone had been easy. Managing it with another person on my shoulder was a whole different ball game.

"It's too late for that. Look." Her voice wavered.

I turned. To my right, back toward the beginning of the course, a wall of flame was heading toward us, funneling up the path.

"Shit!" I said, my mind racing. There was nowhere to go but back where we came from.

Seeing the orange flames behind us, the crocodile turned and dashed into the pond, submerging itself.

The flames roared towards us, leaving us no way back. The heat was searing now, and if I didn't get a move on, the pair of us would be toast.

I staggered forward into a run, but when I rounded the corner around a stand of trees, I pulled up short. A cliff—complete with waterfall—loomed before us. Climbing it while carrying this girl was going to be almost impossible, but what choice did I have?

I stumbled up to the cliff face, but the sandy wall was crumbling, with no firm hand or footholds that I could see.

"There's no way through!" I said, panicking, turning back to see the flames licking dangerously close. The heat threatened to overwhelm me, addling my senses.

"The waterfall," the blonde panted.

I splashed into the water that pooled at the base of the waterfall, but it was too shallow to use as a refuge from the flames. The waterfall drenched us both as I walked through it, dousing us with cool water that stunned me, pulling my thoughts back to our predicament. I pushed behind the water and reached out with one hand before me, but I felt only stone.

My panic mounted as I realized we were trapped. The water falling around us would keep us from burning, but the smoke and heat from the flames were already beginning to scorch my lungs.

We were going to die in this fire, not from the searing heat, but from smoke inhalation. I shied away from the flames, shimmying to the other side of the waterfall, and bumped into something hard sticking out of the rock. My heart fluttered with hope as my hand grasped it. It was a metal rung, fastened to the stone wall at the back of the waterfall.

"Hang on, Blondie," I coughed. "I'm going to need both hands."

Her legs dangled over my front as her head and torso hung behind my back. She put one arm around my waist and the other over my shoulder in an awkward hug.

Now that I had both hands free, I was able to climb the hidden ladder, pulling us both up through the waterfall to the summit. We were dripping wet, and our clothes were black with soot, but we were alive.

I lowered the girl to the ground and peered at the course ahead, stretching my aching back.

From where we were, the vantage was clear, and I could see the rest of the course. This was the highest part, which enabled me to plan a route. In the distance, I could even see the tiny dots of people that had congregated in the parking lot, waiting for the contestants to finish.

Now that we had risen above the fire, I had two choices. Either sit here and wait for help or keep going.

The blonde girl's leg was bleeding freely, and her face was pale. If someone didn't find us soon, she could lose too much blood. If that happened, her death would be on me.

"Come on, Blondie," I said, heaving her back over my shoulders. "We have a race to run..."

5

____

My shoulders ached with the weight of the girl, and my legs felt like lead weights as I pulled her from one obstacle to another. The course would have been difficult on my own, but doing it with an injured person on my back rendered it almost impossible. Each task was designed to break you, to hurt and to push you to your absolute limits, and every time I thought it was okay to stop for a rest, the wall of flame returned, pushing me ever onward.

I mentally thanked all those nights I'd given up to training. Had I not pushed my body then, this course would have been the end of me. Pain and fatigue were my constant companions as I ran, skirting against my absolute limit. At some point along the course, I realized that my words of encouragement to the blonde girl were wasted breath; she'd slipped into unconsciousness. It was just as well, really. I needed to conserve every ounce of energy.

Sweat dripped into my eyes and off my nose as each task became progressively harder. All those weeks I'd spent in John's office as he talked to set designers and technicians and I'd not once thought to look at the plans for the course. I'd wanted to keep it a surprise so I could watch it with fresh eyes. What an idiot. Had I known what was coming, I could have least prepared myself for it.

As it was, I was no more aware of what lay ahead than the other contestants. At the three-quarter point, after dodging a dragon, which thankfully this time did turn out to be animatronic, I literally bumped into one of the other contestants. Despite carrying a person on my back and starting off way behind the others, I'd done something that I hadn't expected to do and actually caught up.

"Where are they?" I screamed at the faerie girl, who looked as surprised to see me as I was to see her. She was stopped at a wall with five doors, deliberating which one to go through. Each door was exactly the same except that each was a different color.

"Where are who?" The young faerie girl asked, looking irked that I'd interrupted her thought process. She must have known she was near the back and therefore unlikely to make it to the actual FFR, but that didn't stop her from throwing shade my way. This was the first time I'd been close to one of the fae since the unfortunate incident—as I'd taken to calling it—in the coffeeshop with the fae prince. I shivered as the air around me seemed somehow displaced. The faerie herself was as close to human looking as fae get, at least a lot closer than some of the weird creatures I'd seen over the past month, but even without seeing her pointy ears, it was easy to tell she was one of them. Her skin had a slight sheen that wasn't altogether natural, and it wasn't just from the sweat of the race. Her eyes, just like the eyes of the male fae had captured my helpless gaze, weren't just dark, they were completely black, and of course, there was the weird feeling of having the air sucked out of me along with the faint crackle of magic.

"The cameras!" I looked all around me. If there were contestants here, surely someone would be filming them?

"Help!" I looked up and cried into the air as the girl went back to contemplating the doors. "This girl is injured. She needs medical help." I didn't even know who I was shouting at anymore, but I did know that if she wasn't seen by a doctor soon, she was in grave danger of suffering permanent damage to her leg, or worse.

"Shut it," the faerie girl snapped at me. "I'm trying to think." She murmured to herself. "It's the yellow door. We saw blue, green, red, and purple flowers along the route, but not yellow. That must be the clue."

"It's the red door," I huffed. I'd seen them from the cliff top above the waterfall and knew that the other doors led to cages. "Can you help me, please? She's unconscious."

"Later, loser," the faerie answered, shoving through the yellow door. Just before it closed, she turned and stuck out her tongue at me.

I furrowed my brow. I'd show her. Taking a deep breath, I kicked my foot out and bashed open the red door. On the other side, the faerie girl glared at me through bars as I hobbled past her.

"Later, loser," I mimicked her words as I passed, though I didn't feel better for it. Petty revenge was not my thing.

I didn't know where all the other contestants were, or if they'd made it through all the obstacles, but I'd passed at least three of them, plus the girl on my back, who wasn't finishing. I wondered how far from the end I was. I let my imagination picture for a moment how amazing it would be if I crossed that finish line among the top six humans. Not that it meant I'd get to join the race.

Summoning the dregs of my strength, I once again set off into the unknown.

The sound of screaming drifted towards me on the breeze, but this time it was no scream of pain. It was the sound of hundreds of people cheering and shouting with excitement as a contestant crossed the line.

The sound spurred me on. I dug deep, quickening my pace.

The finish line came into view ahead of me, a black and white checked banner stretching across the trail above.

As I dashed towards the finish line, I saw three things: the wild crowd cheering me onwards, the ambulance waiting to take Blondie, and John—who was looking daggers at me.

The noise was deafening as I hurdled over the line into the arms of the waiting paramedics, who gently hoisted the girl off my shoulders.

"Nice job Jacq," John clapped me on the shoulder and pulled me away from the cheering crowds.

"Did I place?" I wheezed, my hands on my knees. I was so tired I could barely stand.

"You came in sixth, but that's hardly the point. The contestants were handpicked over the past months—carefully curated by the entire FFR team. They've been through weeks of interviews, tests, and preliminary rounds. You went in there like a bull in a china shop and ruined everything I've been working toward."

"But—" I began.

"You're fired."

I straightened, barely able to comprehend what I'd just heard. "I saved a girl's life!" I argued.

"Save it!" he snapped and stalked back towards the

crowd, leaving me completely alone and for the first time since I'd turned eighteen—out of a job.

AFTER THE LONGEST hottest shower I'd ever taken, I searched the apartment top to bottom for a bottle of Ibuprofen, only to have my search end in an epic failure. I couldn't face leaving the apartment to go to the store, so I settled for downing the only alcohol I could find in the apartment, a quarter of a bottle of Christine's pretentious whiskey, before I fell into bed. Every muscle ached—even some muscles I didn't know I had. Yeah, I was underage, but my parents had always said if I was going to drink they'd rather me do it at home. I figured this qualified.

I closed my eyes and immediately fell asleep. I dreamed about Cass. It was the same dream I always had about her. I watched her go over our backyard fence, as I had countless times before. I called out to her as I always did, begging her not to go. I hadn't done that in real life, but I had in every dream that followed. Usually, I woke up at this point, dripping with sweat and trembling, but this time the dream was different. I opened the window and flew to the ground, chasing after her.

She laughed as she ran away from me, mocking me. She hadn't been laughing in real life, rather she looked frightened. But now she was running and laughing—always out of my reach. The fae male was still with her, at her side as always. I never saw his face in real life and I couldn't now, just the pointy ears peeking out of his thick golden hair. Now he wasn't just holding her hand, he was gripping it possessively. She was struggling to get away from him. Had that happened in real life? I couldn't remember.

I ran as fast as I could to catch up with her, but she remained out of reach. And then the air was sucked away from me, and I couldn't breathe. The male turned. I was going to see his face at last, but I couldn't breathe. I was choking on his magic.

And then I opened my eyes and sucked in a deep breath. My heart raced as I took in my surroundings. I was in my own bed in my own apartment, and apart from the terror running through me, I was all right.

An insistent banging on my door jolted me back to reality and everything that had happened yesterday came back to me. The course. The blonde girl. John's last words to me. I pulled my pillow over my head.

"Go away!" I croaked. Just the effort of it made my head pound. My body had never felt so sore. Even my eyeballs hurt.

"Nope!" Christine opened the door and flung herself on my bed. The motion made me feel sick. Maybe downing that whiskey hadn't been the smartest idea after all.

"I have a famous roomie!" Christine squealed.

"Huh?"

"Come on." She grabbed my hand and dragged me out of bed. My body protested in agony, but I kept my mouth shut. I wanted to know what she was talking about.

She plonked me down on the sofa and turned on the TV.

There I was, running through the trees. I leaned forward, my hand flying to my mouth. A smile crept over me. With the fire behind me and Blondie hanging around my neck, I looked strong. Heroic, even.

"It's on every channel, look." Christine turned the

channel once and then again. She was right. I was all over the news.

"The video's gone viral. Jacq, you're famous!"

I grabbed my phone off the coffee table where I'd abandoned it last night, and goggled. I had twelve missed calls and twenty-seven missed texts. I'd deal with that later. I opened up social media. I had hundreds—thousands of messages. I scrolled through my feed, letting out a little gasp of disbelief.

I was all anyone was talking about. No one cared about the winners. The twelve actual contestants that would compete in the FFR. The media was completely focused on me, and my epic run.

I hadn't been able to find any cameras as I'd gone through the course, but obviously, there'd been plenty of them. They'd caught everything. The crocodile, the flames, the waterfall. Me kicking in the red door, Blondie over my back. I was a meme!

I looked back at the TV in wonder, where a morning talk show host was doing a play-by-play of my route through the course. Excitement rushed though me. Take that, John. Maybe today wasn't shaping up to be so bad after all.

"I'll pour us a celebratory drink," Christine giggled, heading into the kitchen. "Do you know where I put that nice whiskey I got?"

I was saved having to answer by an urgent rapping at the door. I pulled myself off the couch and opened it.

"Jacq, why aren't you at work?" John barked as soon as I opened the door. Behind him, scores of photographers clicked away like hungry locusts, getting hundreds of photos of my shocked and rather hungover expression. I smoothed my messy bun, knowing there was little I could do about my Missoula Rodeo T-shirt and polka dot boxer shorts.

"I...I..."

"I've been trying to call you all morning. Why aren't you answering your phone?"

"I was sleeping," I blustered as John pushed past me into the apartment. Gratefully closing the door on the clicking mass of photographers, I turned to John.

"You're the talk of the town!" He grinned, clasping my shoulders. "I always knew you'd be a star. I can smell talent a mile off."

"You fired me," I reminded him.

"Fired, schmired," He waved a hand. "Jacq. You're in."

I narrowed my eyes, trying to make sense of what he was telling me. "In what?"

"The girl you saved—Brittany Carmine. I doubt you knew, but she just so happens to be the chief exec's daughter. When he saw what you did, he decided to let you go through. Of course, your newfound fame didn't hurt either. The public is crazy over you."

Excitement trilled in me, but caution bloomed even stronger. Things that seemed too good to be true usually were. "But I didn't run the whole course. I didn't go through any of the preliminary rounds. Wouldn't it be unfair to the other contestants?"

John shook his head as though he was talking to a complete simpleton. "This is show biz. Who cares about fair?"

"You must not know Jacq at all," Christine said from the doorway to the kitchen, waving the empty bottle of craft whiskey at me, her eyes narrowed. "She's the epitome of everything fair, except when it comes to polishing off her roomie's alcohol, it seems."

'Sorry,' I mouthed at her and turned my attention back to John.

"Besides, we timed everyone. If you'd started at the same time as everyone else, you'd have placed third, which is a miracle considering you were carrying another person. No one can deny that you deserve to be in that race."

"Oh," I managed, pride welling within me. I knew I had killed that course!

"I know it's a lot to take in, but you need to get packed. The jet leaves from Burbank in three hours."

"Jet?" I said weakly.

John nodded. "The jet that will take the competitors to the training ground in Wales. If you want to go over the Hedge, you better be on it."

John's words finally sank in. Over the Hedge. The Fantastic Faerie Race. I had done it. I was in.

6

———

A sea of hostile faces greeted me as I ducked inside the jet that would take the competitors to the training ground in Wales. I forced my rubbery legs to move me forward and threw my shoulders back. I wouldn't let myself be intimidated by the other competitors, human or fae. I was in the race now. They didn't have to like it, but it wasn't going to change.

I slipped into a seat near the middle of the plane after shoving my duffel bag into the overhead bin. My packing had been a total disaster. What do you bring when you're spontaneously summoned to another continent to prepare for a race in a magical realm? I sure as hell didn't know. Jeans and my toothbrush. That's about as far as I got.

I'd been so caught up in the last-minute dash to the airport that I hadn't even had time to find out who the other competitors were. In the sea of faces that had turned towards me as I boarded the plane, I'd not registered the physical features of their faces beyond their sneers. I wasn't sure I wanted to know even now, but I cast my eyes to the side to see who was closest to me. I felt bad about thinking it, but I hoped it was a human. As it was, it turned out to be an ebony-haired human girl, only a few years older than me. She had her back to me as she was looking out the window.

Her canvas backpack was perched on the seat next to her, covered in patches. One caught my eye. It was from Whitefish Mountain, one of the popular ski resorts north of my hometown. Was she from Montana too? I couldn't help myself. I scooted into the seat by the aisle. "Excuse me," I said.

The girl turned to me. She had the kind of natural beauty that made the rest of us jealous—smooth olive skin, tilted dark eyes rimmed with long black lashes. But that wasn't what struck me. I knew this girl. I cocked my head, sifting through memories. "Genevieve?"

I'd seen her in the trials, of course I had. But it was only now that I was up close to her, that her face clicked into place in my brain.

She let out a little grunt of confirmation. "I wasn't sure if you'd remember me."

I settled into the seat next to her in a flash, moving her bag to the floor. "What are you doing here?"

"I should ask you the same question." She didn't seem as hostile as everyone else on the plane, but she wasn't exactly friendly.

I threw my hands up. "It kinda just happened."

She nodded. "I saw what you did. It was really courageous. But..." she lowered her voice. "You better watch yourself in training. Some of these other competitors aren't happy about you being here. We all busted our asses for weeks to get here, and you just waltzed in."

I swallowed. I wasn't sure I agreed that carrying an unconscious girl through that course from hell was *waltzing in*, but I took her point. "Thanks," I said.

"But seriously, why are you here? Do you still live in Missoula?"

She nodded. "I'm here for the money and the boon, like everyone else. Our coven disbanded after..." she hesitated. *After my sister disappeared*, I wanted to say. She continued. "But I've still been doing magic. I've been learning under our tribe's medicine woman. And getting good. So I thought I'd try my hand, see if I can show these faeries how it's done."

That's right. It was coming back to me. Genevieve was part of the Blackfeet tribe. She had been part of my sister's coven, along with three other girls that my sister had gone to high school with. I used to spy at the attic door, peering through the keyhole as they lit their candles and spoke in strange words. They'd all been questioned by the police when Cass had disappeared, but none of them had known where she'd gone or even the name of the fae male she'd disappeared with. They'd agreed Cass had been acting strange—withdrawn. An image of Genevieve sitting in our kitchen surfaced in my mind—her tear-streaked face blocked by the tan of the sheriff's uniform. A lump grew in my throat, and I was overcome by the urge to grab Genevieve's hand, to touch someone who had touched my sister. It was closer to her than I'd felt in a long time. But I couldn't do that.

I fumbled for a topic that was safe, that wasn't Cass. "I didn't realize medicine magic was the same as...you know... witchcraft." I winced internally at how ignorant I sounded. I knew nothing about magic. I'd stayed as far away from it as possible. Even when Cass and her friends had been dabbling in it all those years ago, I'd stayed clear, preferring the outdoors.

"It is, and it isn't," Genevieve said. "All human magic

uses the same basic principles and the five elements. But the ways to access it can be totally different."

"Human magic?" I asked. "As opposed to..." I trailed off.

"Fae magic?" she said incredulously as if I had just told her I wasn't sure what color the sky was. "God, Jacq, you don't know any of this? You're going to get eaten alive in Faerwild."

"I have a month to train, right?" I said weakly.

Genevieve leaned back against the seat. "You better train your ass off because you can bet that everyone else on this plane knows at least the basic spells."

I swallowed thickly. I didn't even know what the basic spells were, let alone how to cast them.

"Seat belts please," a flight attendant leaned over me. "We'll be taking off soon."

"Thanks," I managed. Genevieve was already closing her eyes, settling in for the long flight. I crept back to my seat across the aisle, trying to ignore the sinking feeling in my stomach and the strange crackle of magic in the air. I had one month. I'd train my ass off. It'd be fine. I'd be fine.

I COULD NEVER SLEEP on flights, so I passed the nine-hour flight watching an action movie marathon and ignoring everyone else. I loved watching the stunts, trying to figure out how they'd done it, trying to imagine all the components that went into getting each shot. To me, this was magic, the way that Hollywood made everything look so real. It was a suitable distraction from my unease, but by the time we landed, I felt strung out from lack of sleep and nerves.

As I was disembarking the plane, I passed between two

fae males conversing in low tones. A jolt of recognition went through me as one of the voices reached my ears. It was the low smooth bass of the guy who had left Blondie bloody in a bear-trap. I craned my head around and froze as my eyes met those of the dark-haired leather-clad male I'd seen the first day of auditions. A shiver went through me, and I ripped my gaze away, hurrying to the exit. I wracked my brain, mentally examining the white-board with contestants' names and faces that had been up in John's office for weeks. Orin Treebaum! That was it. Now I had a name for the asshole who left a poor girl to be eaten by a crocodile. He was one to watch out for.

From the plane, we were hurried onto a bus to take us to Hennington House, where we'd be staying for the month. The huge old house was located outside of the city of Cardiff and had miles of grounds where we'd be training. The house was close to Caerleon, where one of the most famous faerie circles was located. Faerie circles marked portals between the human and faerie world. While the United States had portals, I suspected that John and the other execs wanted the sense of magic and mystery that came with big old castles, foggy moors, and desolate landscapes. At least, that's the only reason I could think of why they'd go to so much trouble to rent a big old house in another country.

I was the last to get off the bus when we arrived in Cardiff, hanging back from the other contestants. So I couldn't have been more surprised when I stepped down from the bus to find the blond fae prince waiting for me. "Americano," he said in his deep purring voice. "Fancy meeting you here."

It was only then that I realized he'd not been on the plane with the rest of us. Being a prince, he probably had a more luxurious way of traveling—like his own private jet.

My face heated as I pushed past him. "That's not my name."

He fell into step beside me but said nothing, as if waiting for something.

"What?" I blurted. His scrutiny made my skin feel too tight—the weird magical aura he projected was too much after hours on a plane and bus.

"I believe human social convention would require you to tell me your actual name at this point," he said with a touch of humor.

"Jacq," I answered, realizing I was coming across bitchier than I intended to. I couldn't help it. These creatures unsettled me. God only knew how I was going to survive being cooped up in a glorified hotel for a month with them.

"I'm Tristam. Nice to meet you." He offered a hand to me, and I looked at it sideways as if it could burn me. He waited a moment longer, and let it drop. "I saw your little run through the obstacle course," he said. "Not bad."

"Thank you." I should be glad that he was being friendly to me, but I couldn't help but be on edge. He was a faerie. He was dangerous.

"If you need any help with your magic, let me know," he said. "I've been told I'm a good teacher."

I gulped. My magical abilities hadn't yet been tested, which was just as well seeing as I didn't have any. I didn't like the way he seemed to already know I was hopeless when it came to magic. Maybe he was only offering to help because I was human, but I wasn't so sure. He hadn't been waiting for anyone else off the bus.

I was saved from answering by the call of a large man with a shaved head who was standing on a step before us, flanked by two other strangers. Hennington House loomed above, lit from below by spotlights that stretched up its rough-hewn flanks. It kind of reminded me of the house from Downton Abbey except with a darker and more foreboding feel about it. I could imagine hundreds of servants moving through its corridors in ye olde days.

"I'm Gabriel," the man was saying. He was wearing an FFR fleece jacket and had his huge arms crossed over his chest. He looked military and had the muscles to prove it. "I'm in charge of you for this month. It's my job to make sure you learn all the skills you need to survive in there. I'll be handling your physical and weapons training. I strongly suggest you pay attention because magic alone won't be enough. On my left is Evaline, who's a Magician of the Third Order. She'll be here to teach you whatever magic you don't yet know. Both human and fae will spend time with her, though the humans among you will get more allotted time for obvious reasons."

The lean blonde woman gave a graceful wave.

"On my right is Niall, who's Cambridge University's foremost expert in fae and the faerie realm. He will be teaching you mortals about what you can expect in there. He was one of the first humans allowed into Faerwild when it opened, and he's written three books on the subject. He's also a World Champion chess player, and is going to teach you to think circles around each other so those riddles and logic games don't kick your ass."

I perked up at that. World Champion chess player? I loved chess. My dad and I had played every Sunday in the winter when the weather was too crappy to do anything. Maybe I could score a game with Niall.

Gabe opened his mouth to speak again when he was

interrupted by an immaculately dressed tall woman, made even taller with the five-inch heels she wore.

"Hello everyone," she purred, stepping right in front of Gabe and not waiting for an introduction.

Gabe moved to one side, his face set in a grimace. "This is Patricia. The humans amongst you might recognize her. She's a TV host."

"Not just any TV host, Gabriel," Patricia admonished, then turned back to us with a wide grin. She reminded me of a cat just about to pounce. "I'm a two-time Emmy winner and the host of the FFR." She let out a giggle that made my stomach turn. "I'll be the one sharing your successes and your defeats with the world. Consider me your biggest cheerleader *and* your worst enemy. Without me, no one on the outside will know what's happening."

As she spoke, a cameraman sidled out from behind her and panned around the contestants. I managed an embarrassed grin as it shone on me for a brief second. I was going to have to work on my TV presence, along with everything else.

"I've got a list of room assignments and your schedule for the month." Gabe jumped in, almost knocking Patricia out of the way. It was clear there was no love lost between those two. "You've all made it through the auditions, but what you don't know is that the audition isn't over. We'll be keeping an eye on you this coming month, and if we think you can't cut it, you won't be going into Faerwild. At the end of the month, you'll team up. How well you do in the next thirty days will determine who gets to pick first. Human's choice. There will be one faerie and one human per team. There will be three trials with three legs of each trial. Between each trial, you'll be awarded a day or two's respite back here before going on to the next trial. The first trial is the Sorcery Trial. That means your magic will be tested right from the start, so you don't want to be skipping your time with Evaline."

My mouth went dry at the thought of being my magic (or lack thereof) being tested.

I looked around at the humans who would be my competition, at the fae who could be my partners. My eyes slid over to Orin, whose arms were crossed tightly over his broad chest, his face unreadable. I shivered. I needed to get to know these competitors, so I could be at the top of the heap when this month ended. So I could take my pick. My eyes met Tristam's, and he grinned. I looked away, my heart leaping in my chest.

"How come the humans get to pick?" One of the fae females asked. I craned my neck to make out the girl who'd been speaking. She had a shock of curly red hair and faint purple tattoos on her face. What kind of faerie was she?

Gabe replied. "You faeries have an automatic edge in this competition. It'll take place on your home turf. The Faerie King and the show producers agreed that letting the humans pick would help even the playing field to some small degree."

The answer seemed to satisfy the girl.

"Mark my words," Gabe said. "The auditions you just completed are going to feel like a walk in the park compared to this month. But if you push yourself, you'll be ready to face whatever comes when you go over the Hedge. What you learn this month could be the difference. Not just between winning and losing but also between living and dying."

7

I nside, the hall was just as magnificent as the outside, and if it weren't for my utter fatigue, I might have taken the chance to take a look around. As it was, when I was shown to my bedroom on the third floor, I fell onto the four-post bed, kicked off my shoes, and slept like a baby.

The wake-up bell for training rang at six a.m. Apparently, the producers wanted to make sure that if the faerie monsters didn't get us, sleep deprivation would. I dragged myself out of my fluffy bed and pulled on a set of FFR clothes that had been left out in my room. Black leggings, white tank top, and a zip-up athletic jacket in the blue and silver of the FFR logo. Apparently, they wanted us all to look the part. But the clothes fit and were comfy, so I didn't complain. My job for the next month was to learn as much as I could and stay out of the way of the other competitors—except when I was kicking their asses on whatever course or test Gabe had concocted for us, of course.

I jogged down the creaky stairs of the house in the direction I hoped would lead me to breakfast. I didn't remember much of the house from last night, I'd been totally exhausted. Looking at it now, it struck me as big, and old, and English, although I'd been schooled not to call anything in Wales "English" by one of the humans on the plane. Wood-paneled walls were hung with faded tapestries while the soaring ceilings were inlaid with gold gilt. The rooms were crowded with ornate furniture that looked too delicate to be used for actual sitting. It wasn't my style, that's for sure, but I couldn't deny the austere decor was beautiful.

I followed the sounds of clinking silverware into a large dining room filled with round tables. The people in the room seemed to take a breath as I darkened the doorway; the other competitors' penetrating gazes swiveled to land on me. I swallowed, ducking my head and heading towards the front where an array of food was set out. Maybe I wasn't so hungry after all. I grabbed a bagel and slathered on some cream cheese before pouring myself a coffee and slipping back out the door.

TRAINING STARTED at seven a.m. Sharp. Despite Gabe's drill sergeant demeanor, I liked him. He seemed to genuinely want to help us. He kind of reminded me of my dad—who had been just as happy showing me how to fillet a trout as do my homework. My heart twisted in my chest. A few of those twelve missed calls yesterday had been from home. When I had a down moment, I needed to call my parents and let them know what was going on.

We lined up to get our instructions for the day, and it was my first chance to scope the competition. The humans, I needed to evaluate—to see how I could beat them. The fae, I needed to evaluate to determine who I wanted to be my partner. *And* how I could beat them. Because only one would end up on my team.

We were a motley bunch. Four human girls—me, Genevieve, a buxom brunette who kept casting barely-veiled glances at Tristam, and a little goth girl with dark eyeliner and bubble-gum pink hair. Two guys—a ripped African-American guy with buzzed hair who looked like a Navy SEAL, and a bearded guy covered in tattoos, who looked like he'd come straight from serving craft cocktails at a hipster bar in Portland. I liked my odds against the lot of them, though the military guy probably had me beat in strength.

And then there were the fae. They were a strange-looking crew. Tristam, who was the closest to "normal" of the lot of them, the red-haired faerie who had spoken last night whose tattoos I was sure had changed, and asshole partner-abandoning Orin, who looked slightly less threatening out of his all black leather attire, but not much.

The other three exuded strangeness and danger in turns. A willowy, tall male with long white hair and pale skin, another devastatingly handsome faerie with black hair and a look that said he knew what hot shit he was, and a small delicate girl with purple hair streaked with sparkles. And unlike the goth girl's pink locks, I had a sneaking suspicion this faerie's look was natural. I really needed to hit the books in faerie class to figure out what the hell I was up against.

Our days were split into four blocks. Physical conditioning with Gabe, weapons training, magic, and study hall. Only the first three were mandatory, the last one was a free period where we could work on what we felt we needed or see Niall to brush up on our Faerie anthropology. I had a feeling I'd be seeing a lot of him. To say my knowledge of Faerwild was inadequate was an understatement, to say the least. I'd learned all I could about it since Cass disappeared, but there was a woeful lack of information about the place. I'd never seen Niall's books. I made a note to find them as soon as I could. Perhaps he had some spare copies.

I thought I'd rather enjoy the training, if not for the other competitors staring at me. And the magic portion, which I wanted nothing to do with. Oh, and the cameras that were everywhere. On second thought, this month was going to suck.

Our first order of business was a jog around the green lawns of the house grounds to get warmed up. I cruised up to the starting line, stretching my legs. I could use a run after being captive in an airplane for half a day.

Tristam sidled up to the line next to me, that Cheshire Cat smile on his face.

I offered a weak smile in return, wishing my knees didn't feel so much like jello when he was around. It wasn't fair, how disarming these faeries were. I needed to keep my eyes on the prize. And remember Cass. Cass. Cass. It would be my mantra this month. She'd be my motivator.

The lawns of the house were flat with flowerbeds decorating the edges before a large red-bricked wall shielded us from the outside world. Beyond that, a dark landscape of low mountains peeked over the top, shadowed by foreboding clouds that threatened to drench us at any point. It was not the mountains I concentrated on now as we all lined up. Even though this was only a warm-up, a nice quick jog around the gardens, I still wanted to prove myself. This was the one part of the training where I knew I could kick ass. I readied myself as the others lined up next to me.

"Go!" Gabe yelled, and the competitors dashed off the starting line.

And it was then that I got my first glimpse of what deep shit I was in.

The purple-haired faerie straight up turned into a white horse—with wings—and galloped out front of all of us. If seeing that didn't give a person pause, I don't know what would. The sexy model-looking faerie sprouted wings from the back of his tank top and flapped into the air while the tall, pale male disappeared ahead so fast I could hardly believe it was real. And then there were the magic users. Orin, Goth-Girl, and Tattoo Guy all did some sort of spell that worked better than a magic mushroom in Mario Kart. In an instant, they were gone. The rest of us mere mortals seemed content to run like normal people, but Navy SEAL and the brunette girl were both off and running like they were competing for Olympic Gold in the 400 meter. I tried to exchange a "can-you-believe-this" look of camaraderie with Genevieve, but she was having none of it, running on ahead like a gazelle. I sighed and dug in, doubling my pace.

Day One. And we were already playing for keeps.

IT PRETTY MUCH GOT WORSE FROM there. The first two blocks of training with Gabe were brutal but manageable. The competitors still seemed determined to impress the judges and cameras with how all-around awesome they were, but it's hard to keep that level of intensity up for twenty-four hours a day. I held my own in weapons training, hand-to-hand combat, archery, and shooting. I killed it in horseback riding, thanks to being raised on a ranch. Magic, not so much.

The first day Evaline took me aside, her smooth, ageless

forehead scrunched in worry. "You didn't do any magic in the auditions. What magic do you know?"

I gave her an apologetic grin and hoped it wasn't a deal breaker. "None?"

She hissed through her teeth and nodded her head. "I feared as much. It is no joke over the Hedge. Everything is magic, from the leaves on the trees to the very water you drink. And everything is trying to kill you. There's no way you'll survive in there if you don't know basic protective enchantments. The first trial isn't called the Sorcery Trial for nothing."

My smile faltered. I was worried about winning. But I hadn't thought about the possibility that someone might die in there. "The producers wouldn't let that..." I trailed off. They'd let me carry an unconscious, bleeding girl around an obstacle course because it made for good television. John had explained to me on the way to the jet that they could have sent a medical team in, but they thought letting me try to save her would improve the ratings. Then I thought of the five-page liability waiver he'd made me sign before getting on the airplane. Maybe I should have read that a bit more closely.

I looked at Evaline. I knew all I needed to know. Magic was dangerous. Magic had stolen Cass from me. But that wouldn't be enough to save me over the Hedge. As much as I didn't want anything to do with magic, if it would keep me alive, let alone give me a fighting chance in the race, I needed to know it. "Teach me," I said.

So she did. "Human magic utilizes five elements—earth, air, water, fire, and aether, which is derived from the stars. It comes from our human soul connection to the cosmos. Faeries don't have souls, not in the same way humans do. They are creatures of the earth, and they use a fifth element called quora. It's much more powerful than aether, and it infuses Faerwild, which is why there's magic everywhere there, even in the plants and animals. Humans can't use quora unless we are utilizing a faerie-enchanted artifact."

"Okay," I said, my stomach flipping. "So how do I make magic from these elements?" I forced out.

"There are many different magical traditions throughout human history. But for your purposes, you need something simple and dependable. And that means spells." She handed me a little leather-bound book. It was inlaid in silver etchings of flowers and vines. It felt heavy and warm in my hand. "This is a grimoire. I want you to try the first spell in the book tonight. Then come back, and we'll discuss it tomorrow."

I nodded my head, feeling slightly sick at the thought of it. I hated magic with a passion, and here I was agreeing to do it. If there was any way I could have done this without it, I would have tried, but I was up against some seriously magical competitors, and I had to survive.

Despite my revulsion to the magical world, I tried the first spell that night—a spell to light a candle. I gathered my bowl of water, my bit of dirt, my candle, and my breath. Feeling foolish, I said the ridiculous words. I must have pronounced them a dozen different ways. But the wick stayed dark. Nothing happened.

I wanted more than anything to be able to light up the room, but in my heart, I knew it was my deep distrust of magic that was holding me back. A desire to win was being driven down by years of avoidance and hatred. It wasn't the magic as such that was my problem; it was my attitude toward it. It was a problem I'd have to work on more than any other part of my training, because without magic, I might as well take the first flight back to LA.

Giving up and throwing the book to one side, I headed out of my room to find Niall. He'd pinned a sign-up sheet to a notice board in the dining room at breakfast, but by dinnertime, there were still no takers. I guess as it was not mandatory, people had decided not to see him, but I needed his knowledge. I was positive Cass was in Faerwild, and if I was ever to find her, I needed to know all that I could.

I found him, his face buried in a book, by a fireplace in a small study. Despite the number of cozy chairs, he was the only one there. When I entered, he looked up and smiled.

"I was beginning to think that my presence here was pointless." He placed his book on a nearby table and beckoned me over. He poured a measure of whiskey into a glass which he held out for me to take. "I don't really condone drinking during competitions, but a wee nip won't harm you." I was surprised until I realized with a little thrill that I was over the legal drinking age in Wales. Nice.

I immediately felt at ease in his company. Taking his offering, I settled into the chair opposite.

"So, what can I help you with? The kind of traps you may find? The obstacles you'll have to overcome? I've not been told exactly what will be in there, but I can give you a broad view of what to expect." His voice was slightly slurred as though the whiskey he was drinking wasn't his first.

"Actually," I began, taking a sip of the amber fluid. "I'd like to learn about Faerwild. What's it like over there?"

"The faerie realm is like no place on earth, but you are asking the wrong question. The Faerwild I know is not the place you'll see. You and the other contestants will be within a giant playing field, so to speak. This portion of Faerwild has been adapted for the race, and is designed to take you to your limit and test you in ways you couldn't possibly imagine."

I nodded. "I want to know about the cities, the towns, all of it."

"Knowing about the cities won't help you, at least not to begin with. You won't even see one until the end of the Sorcery Trial. That much I'm allowed to divulge." He pointed to his nose and nodded his head. "There's not much I'm allowed to tell you, but you can know that."

"Please." It seemed unlikely that Cass would be stuck in any playing field the FFR organizers had designed. Was she free or still some prisoner of the strange blond faerie who had forced her to go? I'd not heard a peep from her since she left, but did that mean she was taken there rather than going of her own free will? But is it really free will if you're threatened, or forced? My dreams of her leaving had gotten worse and worse since I'd found out I was going to be a competitor and now my mind was so messed up that I couldn't remember what was real about the day she left and what my brain had made up to fill in the gaps.

Niall downed his whiskey and poured himself another large measure. He was probably a lot drunker than he first appeared if the bottle was anything to go by. It was half-empty.

"The main city is Elfame, and it's the only one you are likely to see. It's where the Faerie king lives in his palace. That's where they'll take you between trials. It's a beautiful piece of architecture—if you can call it that when it's built by magic. His son lives there too."

Tristam. "Tell me about him."

Niall leaned in like he was sharing a secret. The sharp tang of alcohol tickled my nostrils. "The king is a friend of mine, and though I don't like to brag, the FFR was actually my idea. Just don't let the king hear me say that." Niall winked, though he had mistaken my question. I'd wanted to know about Tristam, not the king. The more I knew about my opponents, the better. At least that's what I told myself.

"What about his son?"

"Which one?"

"He has more than one?" I only knew of Tristam, and I was pretty sure there weren't any other royal family members joining us in the race.

"The king has two sons...well, had two sons. Auberon, the eldest, died a couple of years back. Tristam, you must have met. He is one of your opponents. He's a good lad. Not really much to tell though. He became the crown prince when Auberon died, and I think he finally got a chance to shine. Before that, he lived in his brother's shadow somewhat. He's been trying to prove himself ever since, and I think he joined the FFR to do just that."

"I'd like to read your books if you have any copies available."

Niall's face split into a grin. "It just so happens that I do." He leaned over the arm of the chair, teetering in the process, but managed to retrieve three books from the floor. He handed them to me. "These will give you a thorough overview of Faerwild. I'm not sure how helpful they will be in the race itself, but they should apprise you of the type of people and creatures you'll encounter."

Then he frowned. "Actually, these are my personal copies, with some notes in the margins." He blinked quickly as if trying to focus. He reached out to grab the books back from me, but I moved them out of the way of his clumsy swipe.

"Please, I'd really like to read them," I stood, cradling the books to my chest. Now I was curious about what he didn't want me to see. Was it something that would give me a leg up in the race?

He seemed to consider and finally waved a hand. "It's just mindless natter I suppose. Ramblings of a scholar about the brotherhood and such."

"Great, thank you," I said, eager to leave before he changed his mind. "Thanks for the whiskey," I threw over my shoulder as I hurried out of the study.

Back in my room, I picked up the grimoire I'd thrown on the floor in a huff and put it at the side of my bed with the three new books.

Tomorrow after training, I was going to have a lot of reading to do.

The next morning at breakfast Gabe walked in looking particularly tense. Marching right past us, he headed to the buffet and turned to address us.

"Contestants," he began loudly. There was a clatter of cutlery as people turned their attention away from their breakfasts. "I'm afraid I've got some bad news for you. Niall was taken sick last night and has headed home to Ireland. It shouldn't affect anyone's training. You still have myself and Evaline, but if you have any concerns, you may ask me directly."

There was a silence as we took the news in. He'd been fine last night albeit a little worse for wear for all the whiskey he'd consumed. I wondered if that was the real reason he'd left. Perhaps he'd been found drunk and sent home. My mind wandered to the books upstairs. At least he'd given me those before leaving.

After breakfast, I headed back upstairs to collect my FFR jacket as the weather had taken a turn for the worse. Something about the way Niall had been so secretive the night before and now his mysterious absence made me want to check the books out now. He'd mentioned something about writing in them which made me wonder if it was somehow connected to him leaving. When I opened my door and checked the nightstand, only the grimoire was there. I checked around the floor and even under my bed, but I already knew they were gone. Someone had been in my room.

8

____

Over the next weeks, Niall's disappearance became less of a talking point as everyone hunkered down into their training. Mine was going as badly as it could possibly get. Evaline grew increasingly frustrated with me and I with her. We sat together for hours. She took over my study hall. We tried shaman magic, we tried djinn magic, we tried meditation and crystals and chakra alignment and chanting until I felt like I was living in a new age shop. Nothing worked. I didn't know whether I was relieved or terrified to be going into Faerwild without a lick of magic. Both I guess.

But for better or worse, it seemed that I was the only human Evaline had ever come across that had zero magical ability. And it seemed there was nothing we could do to change it.

It didn't help that the fae used magic at every given opportunity. Whether they were just doing it to show off for the cameras that tracked our every move or if it was so ingrained into them that they couldn't survive without it, I didn't know, but it was seriously beginning to get on my nerves. If they weren't floating down the corridor, they were making things appear out of thin air. I was still waiting to see one pull a rabbit from a hat, but it had to happen. Any day now!

I sat eating my breakfast alone as I had every morning since arriving when a newspaper was dropped on the table in front of me. Without even glancing at it, I looked up to see who thought it was a good idea to interrupt me during breakfast.

Patricia slinked into the seat beside me, her crimson lips turned upward in a semblance of a smile. I'd done my best to ignore her for the past month. Unlike many of the others who courted fame, I'd taken every step necessary to stay out of its path. Fame didn't interest me, nor did the prize money. There was only one reason I wanted to go into the faerie realm, and I didn't particularly want anyone else to know that. I figured it was easier to stay away from Patricia and her shadow, the cameraman, than come up with some lie.

But, as she'd sought me out and I was kinda cornered, I picked up the paper and offered her an interested if not confused expression.

"Darling," she mewled, taking the newspaper out of my hands and turning to page eight where there was a photo of me looking miserable next to the other competitors. I remembered the day it was taken, less than a week previously. Gabe'd had us training in the rain all morning, and I'd failed to light that effing candle yet again. "How can you not know anything about the media? You are from Hollywood aren't you?"

I nodded suspiciously.

"When you came here, you were topping the polls. You were the hero of the hour, and everyone was rooting for you. A month of looking at that soggy, miserable face of yours, and you are now hovering at the bottom of the popularity ranking."

"Oh," I replied noncommittally. I didn't give a crap how popular I was. I wasn't going for prom queen here. Not that I could compete with pink-haired women or blonde weirdoes who could disappear by magic and reappear at will, usually right in front of me in the breakfast line. And unless Penn and Teller were planning on paying me a visit in the next few days to give me a crash course, I was never going to.

"You know, if you wore a little make-up, you'd look as good as those fae girls and even better than some of the humans. Maybe if you smiled a little too," Patricia suggested, reaching a hand out to try to grasp a strand of my ponytail that was hanging over my shoulder.

I jerked back, trying to control the anger bubbling up inside me. I couldn't see the cameraman anywhere, but that didn't mean he wasn't around. Snapping at the woman hosting the show wasn't going to win me any brownie points, as much as it might make me feel better at the moment.

"I'm not here to win a popularity contest," I hissed, deliberately keeping my voice low. I could see some of the other contestants looking my way out of interest. "The only competition I'm interested in winning is the Fantastic Faerie Race."

That wasn't true either, but I was hardly going to tell her that the only reason I was here was to get into Faerwild to find my sister.

Patricia leaned in towards me, her flowery perfume making my stomach churn. "But you won't win if you don't know any magic."

I sat back in my seat and folded my arms. "Who said I don't know any magic?"

The tall white-haired fae, the one who'd stolen my place in the breakfast line and nabbed the last croissant, Yael was his name, snickered and I realized I'd not been as quiet as I hoped. My lessons with Evaline had been private, and I trusted her not to tell anyone about my lack of abilities in that field, but I could hardly hide it when the others were always showing off theirs.

"Maybe you're a dark horse and know more than you are letting on, but maybe—and I suspect it's more likely—you can't do magic at all," Patricia said. "If that's the case, the studio execs are going to cut you."

"Excuse me?" I recoiled. Cut me?

"It doesn't matter to me one way or another," she remarked, checking the polish on her nails, "but I thought it would be nice to have a fellow L.A. girl going in there and winning. It will make good TV either way."

"What will?" I didn't like what I was hearing one bit.

"Tomorrow is your final day of training. You'll be asked to prove your magical ability. If you don't show anything... well, it's a third of the competition. They'll replace you with someone else from the auditions. Someone who really deserves it."

Patricia stood up and left me with my cornflakes and a feeling of dread in the pit of my stomach. No one had said anything about a test. Up until now, I'd not really been too bothered about the stupid TV show as once I was in Faerwild, I was planning to make a run for it. But if I couldn't pass some stupid test, I might not even get in there at all.

I left my cereal half-eaten and rushed out of the dining room to find Evaline. I found her outside in the garden meditating.

"You never told me there was a test!" I shouted at her angrily.

She held one finger up to silence me and took a deep breath before exhaling loudly and opening her eyes.

"Jacq, how nice to see you."

"Don't!" I spat. "You should have told me."

She picked herself off the floor where she'd been sitting cross-legged and walked over to me.

"I didn't know about a test until this morning. I'm sorry Jacq. I didn't hide anything from you. There was a meeting last night about your lack of progress. The fact is, you didn't audition. The only reason you were here was because the public loved you. But with your lack of progress, the viewers back home have lost interest. If you can't even garner interest as the underdog, there's not much reason to send you in, over someone who is a real competitor. I'm sorry."

I kicked a flower and watched its blossom sail through the air. I'd been so intent on keeping my head down and out of the limelight that I'd not considered how it would look to those watching on TV.

"Please help me," I begged her. I needed to pull something out of the hat by tomorrow morning, or I was out.

She put her hand on my shoulder and looked at me through kind brown eyes.

"Jacq. You aren't magic. I'm sorry, but you aren't. If I were you, I'd spend the day sucking up to the cameras and being as interesting as possible so that execs can't let you go. You'll not get far over the Hedge, but at least you'll make it in there if you can woo the public again." With that, she turned back towards the house.

I walked through the gardens slowly, my mind spinning. I was more likely to pull a bunch of chrysanthemums out of my ass than become popular again in a day. I'd spent the best part of the month avoiding the cameras and had made no effort to be 'interesting' when they were around. What an idiot I'd been! If I knew Hollywood, and I did, anything amazing I did today would come across as insincere, and the public would hate me more.

"Penny for your thoughts?"

I looked up to find Tristam. He really was extraordinarily beautiful, but as with the other fae, I'd kept my distance. Even without the whole Cass mess, the fae just creeped me out, and the magical energy they put off gave me a headache, like the difference in magical pressure between them and the human world just set my teeth on edge. When I didn't speak, he darted a graceful hand behind my ear and brought a penny out.

I snorted. "My dad used to do that trick on me and my sister when we were kids," I said, then mentally kicked myself for mentioning Cass. He didn't pick up on it.

"I bet he didn't really conjure the penny out of thin air, though, did he?" Tristam asked in his easy-going manner.

"No, human fathers don't generally have that ability. He hid the coin between his fingers," I explained the trick. "It was usually a chocolate coin though."

Tristam handed me the coin, and the second it hit my palm, it turned into a chocolate bar.

Despite my misery, I couldn't help but let out a laugh.

"It's nice to see you smile. I get the impression you aren't too happy to be here."

I unwrapped the chocolate and sniffed at it. It looked real. I took a bite. It was good—dark chocolate with toffee bits.

"I want to be here," I said, swallowing. "I really want to be here, but I guess I've been a little too focused. According to Patricia, I'm not interesting enough for the "viewers" without a bunch of fancy magic tricks and...fake chocolate." I sighed.

"Hey, that's real chocolate," he said.

"If I don't suddenly become a whole lot more interesting, they're going replace me." I don't know why I was telling him this. I guess it was because I had no one else to talk to. Some of the others had formed alliances of sorts, but I'd been the loner of the group from day one. Well, me and Orin. He didn't seem to talk to anyone.

"You know what would spice things up a bit? Some illicit romance. Tonight at dinner, storm across the dining room and kiss me within an inch of your life." From his broad grin, I couldn't tell if he was being genuine or messing with me.

My face heated. "Keep dreaming. Besides, I doubt another human throwing herself at the faerie prince counts as newsworthy."

"Fine," he countered. "Throw yourself at Orin. That'd make for some interesting TV."

"Orin!" I shuddered. "He'd probably turn me into a toad or something."

"Actually, we can't do that," Tristam said with a grin.

"See, that's my problem." I threw up my hands.

"What problem?"

I hesitated, glancing around me to make sure we were alone. None of the contestants knew about my complete lack of magic skills. I didn't want to appear to be the weak one of the group, but at this late stage, what did it matter? He had offered to help me, our first day here. Maybe, conceivably, the offer had been genuine. I took a deep breath and plunged ahead. "I can't do magic."

Tristam arched a brow. Did he have to be so damn good looking? "None at all?"

I shook my head, praying I hadn't just made a huge

mistake, that he wasn't going to use this to his advantage. "If I don't either become the talk of the show or prove my magical ability by tomorrow, they're going to boot me out of here."

In the distance, a horn went off, marking the start of our time with Gabe.

Tristam didn't say another word as we walked back to the stretch of lawn where we worked out. The others were already there preparing for the last day of practice. I joined them, but my heart wasn't in it. What was the point being brilliant at everything Gabe had to show me if I was going to be on the first plane back to L.A. tomorrow?

By dinnertime, I still had no idea what to do. I looked over at Tristam who lifted both brows at me. I shook my head at him, telling him there was no way I was going to create a scene by rushing over there and kissing him. He nodded towards Orin with a sly grin, to which I shook my head even harder.

I took my plate and headed up to my room to eat. I wasn't in the mood to socialize.

Outside, the sun lowered in the sky, leaving my room dark as dusk fell. I was too miserable to even turn on the light. Although, as I had every night, I pulled out the grimoire and the candle and began to recite the nonsense words. I'd only been at it for a couple of minutes when I heard a knock on my door. Not caring if anyone saw my pathetic efforts anymore, I left everything out on the floor and opened the door.

I was shocked to see Tristam standing there; I'd been expecting Patricia ready to tell me to pack my bags. He cocked his head to look over my shoulder, taking in the grimoire and magical items on my floor. Without asking my permission, he grabbed my hand and pulled me from my room. It was so unexpected; I did nothing to stop it. "Come with me."

As if he'd left me any choice in the matter. He wasn't holding my hand with much force, but there was something compelling me to stay by his side. I could feel his energy running through me, right up my arm and I wondered if this was the quora that Evaline had mentioned. It was different from the innate energy I felt around the fae. This was much more interesting.

"Where are we going?" I whispered as he took me through deserted corridors then up a flight of stairs to the top floor.

"You'll see."

We stopped at a door with a lock. He did something with his hand, and the door opened. As soon as it did, a gust of wind hit me in the face along with something wet.

"Is this magic?" I asked, shielding my face from the wind.

Tristam laughed. "No. It's outside. I'm taking you up to the roof." He closed the door behind him and cast a spell to lock it again. I wondered briefly if he planned to throw me off it. At least, that way I'd be interesting, I thought blackly.

The rain lashed down as it had almost every day I'd been here, but this time, it was accompanied by the roaring of thunder. A flash lit up the sky, making me jump. In the distance to my right, I could see the lights of Cardiff, but to my left, the dark mountains made me feel like we were already over the Hedge. It didn't help that Tristam had performed a spell stopping the rain directly above our heads. All around, a gale blew and rain pelted down, but the pair of us remained dry in Tristam's protective magical bubble. He pulled a candle from his pocket and placed it on the stone tile in the center of the circle.

"What is this?" I shivered, not because I was cold, but because there was something deeply thrilling about an illicit rendezvous on the roof of a Welsh mansion in the middle of a storm with a faerie prince. The thought chilled me more than the cold gusts of wind. Was this what Cass had felt when she had first met the faerie who had taken her? Special. Electrified. Alive.

"Light the candle," commanded Tristam as he sat down on one side of it.

"I can't. The grimoire is downstairs in my room, and the dirt is there," I protested.

Tristam shook his head and laughed. "Dirt?"

I prickled. He was mocking me. Yet...he'd brought me up here for a reason.

"Will you sit down? Look at the candle."

I stifled a sigh as I folded my legs beneath me and did what he said. It wasn't the same candle I'd used downstairs, but it may as well have been. It was ordinary, just like I was. Looking at the damn thing was having no effect whatsoever. I began to chant the magic words I'd memorized under my breath.

"Stop. You don't need to speak for this. Just look at the candle."

I glared at the stupid thing as Tristam stood and walked around me, crouching down behind me. I could feel the tickle of his breath on my ear. "Feel the warmth within you."

"It's freezing!" I pointed out.

"Forget the weather. Feel the warmth in your very soul, right at your core."

If I had any warmth in me right now, it was a direct result of him whispering in my ear. Still, I tried to focus on the candle.

"It is not the candle that is magic," he coached. "It is the flame. Feel that warmth in you and magnify it."

I concentrated on the warmth in my belly and imagined myself on Santa Monica Beach on a hot July day. I thought of sunburns and hot tubs and the fires my high school friends and I roasted s'mores over. No longer did my fingertips feel the stinging bite of the cold Welsh weather. Warmth permeated my body.

"Keep the energy going," Tristam whispered, and my temperature increased a few more degrees. I could feel beads of sweat begin to trickle down my face as the heat inside me began to burn.

"I can feel it!" I marveled. "I'm not cold anymore."

"Now compact it. Take all that energy and make it small. Imagine it as a speck of light... a laser-sharp dot of heat." I did as he said and cried out with the pain of it.

"Now!" he yelled. "Shoot it to the wick!"

I closed my eyes and expelled the burning energy, pressed it away from myself. Then I felt Tristam's arms under mine, and he was pulling me back.

I opened my eyes as the rain once again dripped onto my hot face, steam rising as the cold droplets hit my fevered skin. I peered through the thick rain at where the candle flame should be. Nothing. My spirits sank. I'd failed again. Without the heat I'd built up, the cold once roared back in, sending a wracking shiver through me.

"What happened?" I asked wondering why he'd pulled me back.

"Oh, nothing. You only went and set the roof on fire. I had to pull you away from it to stop you from getting burned."

I opened my mouth in shock. I'd seen no fire, but as he

led me closer to where we had been sitting, I saw the black scorch marks with a mess of wax in the middle.

"I did magic?" My lips curled up into a grin as I realized what I'd done.

"You did magic!" Tristam grinned back. "Look at your hand. It's still glowing slightly with the aftereffects of the magic. Just do me a favor. Don't accidentally set the judges alight tomorrow. I don't think they'd appreciate it."

I looked down, and sure enough, the veins under my skin glowed slightly. As I watched with awe, they slowly dimmed to normal.

I threw my arms around Tristam, squeezing with all my might. My distrust of faeries be damned. He had helped me. He just might have saved me. The rain fell around us, soaking us to the skin, but I didn't care.

Excitement filled me as I walked slowly back to my room. The light in the halls of Hennington House were dim thanks to the late hour, but it was enough for me to fumble my way back to my room.

I'd almost made it back when a shadowed figure at the end of the corridor caught my eye. My first thought was that someone had found out what I was up to, but I pushed it to the back of my mind. I didn't want to be caught being up so late practicing magic, but whoever was at the other end of the corridor looked like they didn't want to be caught either. I flattened myself against a wall, hidden among the shadows and watched as they crept down the corridor towards me. I'd not been spotted, but if they got any closer, they'd see me. Panicked thoughts of reasons I would be out of bed at such a late hour flittered through my mind, but I needn't have worried. Whoever it was stopped in front of a door, and quiet as a mouse, opened the door and stepped inside.

Letting out a long breath, I tiptoed down the corridor. The door they'd stepped through had a sign on it. Even in the darkness, I could read it clearly. It was a cleaning closet. Who would be creeping around in the middle of the night and hiding in a cleaning closet? From inside, I could hear the muffled voices of two people conversing. A man and a woman. Stepping closer to hear what they were saying, I felt a crunch underfoot. Beneath my shoe was a single earring in the shape of a thistle and rose. Picking it up, I put it in my pocket, smelling the faint scent of flowery perfume. I decided to leave whoever was in the closet alone. For all I knew, a couple of the contestants were having a clandestine hookup and it really wasn't any of my business. I walked to the end of the corridor and headed into my own room where I flopped onto the bed. I'd done magic! I was back in the race.

9

The next morning I hopped out of bed bright and early feeling excited about what the day would bring. Now that I had the ability to perform magic, I wasn't going to be replaced. Today we picked our partners. Today was the day I was going to enter the Faerwild for the first time.

I took my candle and copied what I'd done last night, imagining the hottest places I'd been. I could feel the energy inside me, but try as I might, I couldn't emulate what I'd done the night before.

I spent an hour, but nothing worked.

By the time the breakfast gong rang out, I was in a state of panic. I pocketed the candle and ran downstairs to speak to Tristam before anyone else did.

I found him in the dining room talking to Sophia, one of the other humans. She was almost as tall as him with long wavy hair and a perfect face. Even from this distance, it was easy to see she was flirting with him. She'd shown up to the lessons every day in flawless makeup and spent most of the time pouting into the camera for her million plus fan base on Instagram.

I can't say I cared much for her, but I wasn't prepared for the pang of jealousy I felt as she ran her perfectly manicured hand down Tristam's arm.

I shook it off, annoyed at myself and waved at him, hoping he'd take the hint and come my way.

He whispered something in Sophia's ear, causing her to giggle before he made his way over to me. I dragged him out into the corridor peering both ways to make sure we were alone.

"I can't do it!" I hissed.

"What?"

"The magic. I've been trying all morning, and the candle won't light." I pulled it out of my pocket and showed it to him as if to prove my point. He took the candle and made it disappear into thin air. "The candle isn't the magic one. You are," he reminded me.

"I'm not! They'll throw me out!"

I closed my mouth as a willowy young woman walked past us into the dining hall.

"Who is she?" I asked before feeling the clap of a hand on my shoulder and the cloying scent of flowers.

"Your replacement," Patricia said. "They flew her in this morning. She'll be taking your spot unless you do something spectacular today." With that encouraging sentiment, she flashed me a fake smile which made my stomach churn even more than it already had been.

"Ah, I wondered where that went." She bent down, picking something off the floor and pocketing it in the pocket of her impeccably tailored pantsuit. I saw what it was before it disappeared—the earring I'd picked off the floor the night before. It must have fallen out of my pocket when I pulled out the candle. So it was Patricia who was secretly meeting someone in the cleaning closet. What on earth was she up to? She gave Tristam and me a wink and followed the girl into the dining hall.

A smile quirked at the corner of Tristam's perfect mouth. *Stop looking at his mouth*, I schooled myself.

"Last chance for the kiss angle...I'm game if you are."

"This isn't a joke!" I hissed at him, whirling and pushing out one of the doors into the garden. I knew I needed to eat, but I felt sick with fear. The lawns were now surrounded by a large fence and I saw a number of people in suits walk in through a small gate followed by Patricia and her cameraman. Seconds later, she walked back out alone and stalked to the edge of the fence, disappearing around it. There was definitely something suspicious going on with her, and the more I thought about it, the less I suspected that she'd been hooking up with any of the contestants. It must be something else.

Pulling myself up from the wall, I elected to follow her. Anything to take my mind off my impending failure. Peeking around the fence, I saw her deep in conversation with a man with thick facial hair and an unruly appearance. They were speaking in hushed tones, but I was close enough to pick up a little of what they were saying.

"What about the Brotherhood?" the man asked before he was hushed by Patricia. She handed him something, but with her back to me, I couldn't see what it was. The man looked around quickly, causing me to duck back. I breathed in quickly, finally recognizing him. He looked a mess, and most of his face was hidden by his beard, but it was definitely him. Niall. What was he doing back here and why was he hiding away, talking to Patricia? It must have been him she was meeting in the cleaning closet.

"What are you doing?" someone behind me asked.

My heart jumped into my throat, and I nearly fell over as I spun around. It was Orin.

"Not cheating are you?" he said coldly.

Taking a deep breath, I pulled myself up to my full height, ready to tell him where to go—when Patricia walked past us.

Orin eyed her suspiciously before walking around me and peeking around the fence where Patricia had just emerged.

I followed suit. Niall was gone. He must have hopped over the wall at the end of the garden.

Stepping past Orin, I headed back to the low wall and plonked myself on it, watching the comings and goings of the FFR staff until all the other contestants were lined up. Then I reluctantly dragged my feet to my spot in line.

Out of the corner of my eye, I watched the willowy girl chatting freely with one of the show's producers.

Patricia walked over to us. She had even more makeup on than usual, and that flowery scent she wore was stronger than ever. I wanted to ask her why she was having secret meetings with Niall, but the cameras had already begun to roll.

"Good luck everyone." She turned to the camera. "This is it. Inside the fence sit three judges, including Vale Oban-stone himself, king of Faerwild. Each contestant has to prove their worth in strength, fighting skill, magic, or logic. How the human contestants do in this final test will deter-mine their ranking for the purpose of choosing teammates. How the faerie contestants do will help our dear humans decide who's the strongest partner to pick. The current rankings are as follows: in the lead, Phillip Ryan of Alberta,

Canada." I listened woodenly as she announced the rankings. Phillip—that was the tattooed guy.

"Genevieve Running Deer of Helena, Montana." Genevieve had been killing it in training, so I was happy for her. Sort of.

"Sophia Hernandez of Puebla, Mexico." Or Tristam's number one fan...

"Molly Rhodes of Manchester, England." Goth girl.

"Duncan Riker of Phoenix, Arizona." Or Navy SEAL, as I'd dubbed him.

I closed my eyes against the embarrassment as Patricia announced my name last. "Jacqueline Cunningham, of Irvine, California." She said the word Irvine with a twinge of distaste. Sorry, I can't afford to live in WeHo on a gopher salary, I wanted to gripe.

Patricia was handed a small red velvet bag. Out of it— her movement exaggerated for drama—she pulled a small stone, which she then showed to the camera.

"First up is Orin!"

Orin stood sulkily and entered the fence, disappearing into the enclosure where the final tests would take place. How was it that the people watching on TV didn't like me but liked him? The guy was a total creep that never once cracked a smile. He was only in there a couple of minutes before a buzzer went off and Patricia was once again rummaging around in her velvet bag. I waited for Orin to emerge, but as Sophia's name was called, it was clear that Orin was staying inside.

Each time a name was called, my stomach twisted in knots, but near the end, there was only Tristam and I left outside. Some of the others had only been in there a few seconds before the buzzer sounded. The girl with the pink hair had been the longest at fifteen minutes.

Patricia pulled out a stone, and I held my breath. "Tristam!"

"Good luck!" I whispered as he left the bench. He didn't need luck. His father was the one judging him, so I was surprised when the buzzer didn't ring immediately. I timed him on my watch. Nine minutes and thirty-five seconds to complete his task. He took the longest of all the fae to finish.

Then it was my turn. Patricia talked about me to the camera, but I ignored her as I walked to the gate, my ears burning.

I'd never been so nervous in my life as I was when the gate opened, but the inside was not as scary as I expected. If anything, the set up was mundane—with a long table at the end with the judges and a bench at the side with my fellow competitors. I guess they were allowed to stay and watch once they had finished.

The purple-haired fae girl gave me a nod and a smile as I walked forward. I'd never spoken to her, but it seemed she was cheering me on. That was nice.

Next to her Tristam nodded almost imperceptibly.

"Your Majesty!" I bowed to the king and gave a smaller nod to the judges on either side of him. One I recognized as a jaded pop star who'd been huge in the nineties before falling into obscurity only to revive her career with stints on television show panels like this one. On the other end, was a famous nasty man of TV. He was known as an alcoholic womanizer, and the public loved to hate him. What they didn't know was that after every show he appeared on, he washed off his fake tattoos, and went home to his husband Bryan and his two corgis. Despite how he came across on TV, he didn't have a mean bone in his body. Christine had been to his house with one of her more famous actor friends for a private yoga session with fifty of his closest friends.

The Faerie king, Tristam's father, wasn't as intimidating as I'd expected. He was preternaturally handsome like Tristam and wore a perfectly tailored slate gray suit with a subtle stripe. Not the cloak and velvet tunic I had imagined. There was a raw sense of power about him—I swore I could almost feel his magic from where I was standing. But besides that, he didn't seem much different from the studio execs I worked around.

At either side of the judge's table, two cameras pointed at me, both with their red lights on. I took a deep breath, waiting to see what they had in store for me.

"Your task is simple," the king said. His voice was deep and calm but somehow still managed to make me shiver. He *was* one of the most dangerous males in this realm or over the Hedge. "I want you to take this apple from my hand." He held his arm out. I hesitated, wondering what the catch was. I was only a few steps from him. To my right and behind me I heard someone groan. I had a feeling it was Tristam.

I stepped forward and held out my own hand. When my fingertips were an inch away from the apple, he disappeared.

The contestants jeered, causing me to turn. The king stood in the far end of the fenced-in area, a smile on his face and the apple still in his outstretched hand.

I glanced over at the contestants. Tristam had his head in his hands.

I didn't know what to do, but I was aware that the cameras were running and the studio was looking for an excuse to get rid of me. Maybe I couldn't use magic, but I *could* run.

I raced toward him, pelting at top speed, but as soon as I was near, he'd disappear, ending up somewhere else within the fence. I carried on running, chasing him from spot to spot, hoping I'd catch him before he had a chance to move. After a good ten minutes, I knew I was losing. I'd run around the inside of the fence what felt like a hundred times, and I'd not come close to grabbing the apple.

"Use magic!" I heard Molly with the pink hair say in a singsong voice, and the others broke into peals of laughter. They knew my secret. I couldn't do this.

The king himself gave a little chuckle, which pissed me off. I strode over to him forcefully, crossing the grass. This time I didn't run but kept eye contact. I could feel my anger burning inside as everyone around me laughed.

"Give me the apple!" I shouted when I was a foot away from him. I held out my arm and concentrated. All around me people stopped laughing, and all I could hear was silence. The king looked at me through mocking eyes, as if daring me to come closer. I knew if I took one step nearer to him, he'd be gone again, and I'd be left chasing him until the studio decided enough was enough. I thought of Cass, and my anger intensified. I hated the fae, and he was the king of all of them. The king who was currently mocking me.

"Give me the apple!" I repeated, this time a little louder.

"Why don't you make me, human?" His words were amused. He was enjoying this.

The apple was less than a foot from my hand. I concentrated the anger into a pinprick as Tristam had shown me. It burned my insides as I thought about all the time that had gone by since I last saw Cass. Then in a rush of energy, I pushed it out of me, concentrating on the apple. It wavered a bit in his hand which caused him to stiffen, but the apple remained steadfastly where it was.

Until a jet of purple light flew up from the ground, knocking his hand and sending the apple flying into the air.

I leaped up and grabbed the apple. In front of me, the king stared at me in shock as the buzzer sounded. My heart thumped in my chest as I realized I'd made it through. Relief warred with excitement and trepidation. I was going in!

It was only a few seconds later when my excitement had died down that I thought about what had happened. There was no doubt in my mind that I'd made the apple move a little, but the more I thought about it, I couldn't see how I'd made the purple light. I hadn't felt a power coming from me, not like I had when I'd lit the fire on the roof. I turned to the rest of the contestants to join them, and it was then that I noticed Tristam.

He pulled his hand back quickly and shoved it in his pocket, but I'd already seen it. He winked at me.

The veins in his hand glowed purple. It wasn't me who had moved the apple after all. It was Tristam.

10

———

I'd hardly had time to think about what had just happened when Patricia waltzed to the front, cue card in hand. "I have here the new rankings for the Fantastic Faerie Race. The top human competitor will have first pick of our fabulous fae competitors." I could almost hear the tense music they'd be playing over the scene as it was broadcast.

"The first competitor to choose is...Genevieve Running Deer!"

I was happy for her. At least one Helena girl could represent, even if I'd been a serious embarrassment in the last task. Cass would be proud.

Genevieve stepped up. "I choose Zee Morningfire," she said. It was the red-haired girl with the purple tattoos on her face. I'd found out she was half-salamander, a fire elemental. She was a serious competitor. Good pick, Gen, I thought.

"Next is Phillip Ryan!"

He rubbed a tattooed hand across his beard as if considering. It was for show. I'm sure all of us had decided exactly who we wanted as our partner, and in what order. Not like

I'd get to choose. I was pretty sure I'd still be last. It was like fifth-grade gym class all over again. Except I'd killed it in gym. I'd always been picked first. Stupid magic.

"I choose Dulcina Silver," he said. Also a smart choice. The purple haired Pegasus shifter. He could just make her turn into a horse and fly them through Faerwild. I suppressed a pang of jealousy.

"Our next competitor is Sophia Hernandez!"

Sophia stepped up and waited about one-millisecond before declaring her choice, "Tristam Obanstone." She beamed at him, and I had to hold back an eye-roll. But I probably would have picked him too, if I were her. Besides his looks, he was the king's son. Surely, he'd have some sort of leg up in the race.

"Duncan Riker!" Patricia called.

Duncan swaggered to the front of the stage. "Yael of Barr Sliebhe," Duncan nodded his head towards the impossibly tall pale faerie. I didn't know much about the faerie male beyond his croissant-stealing abilities. If I was honest, he creeped me the hell out. Well, most of them did. The strange aura around the fae was faintest with Yael—as if he was barely even there. Which seemed in keeping with his ability to pop in and out and scare the crap out of me.

That left two. Pink-haired Molly and me. And two faeries. The impossibly handsome Ario Lazer, whom I had learned was an incubus—um yeah, apparently, that was a real thing —and Orin. I shivered as I looked at him, his black gaze cast down, his jaw set. He hadn't done poorly in training. If anything, he had kept up with the rest. But his broody silence and death-glares had kept everyone from approaching him. He was the only one I hadn't seen performing magic. Not any at all. He must be able to because he was quick to finish his tests, but he kept his talents...or lack thereof, well hidden. He was an average competitor, but a world-class asshole. And because of it, he would be picked last.

Horror overtook me as I realized what was about to happen.

"Molly Rhodes!" Patricia said, ushering Molly to the front.

I could practically mouth the words with her. "I choose Ario Lazer," Molly said with a giggle. Ario swaggered over, throwing an arm around her shoulder, grinning and baring two pointed canines. Ugh. Those two deserved each other.

"That leaves our final competitor," Patricia said. She seemed surprised when she read the card, but hadn't I lived up to their little test? I either had to wow them or do magic. And I had done magic. Or, they thought I had, anyway. "Jacqueline Cunningham."

I stepped up, my words catching in my throat. I couldn't bring myself to look at him, to face the frosty stare I knew was shooting my way. "Orin Treebaum," I said, the words feeling like a yoke settling around my neck.

Orin and I walked stiffly to our spot on the stage as the cameras panned across the teams. These were my competition if I wanted to get the king's boon and get Cass back. And Orin, for better or worse, had just become my only ally.

THE PRODUCERS WASTED no time shuttling us from Herrington House to Caerleon, where we'd pass through the faerie circle into Faerwild. It seemed we were to go everywhere with our teammate now, so I was stuck with Mr. Crabbypants, as I had unceremoniously named Orin. There had been nothing but stony silence between us on the bus ride, and now that we were turning off the highway, I thought I would scream just to hear something. "Listen," I turned to him, shaking my head. This was stupid. We'll have to learn to work together. "You weren't exactly my first choice either, okay?" I said. Best get it out there. "But we're going to have to make the best of it."

"Agreed," he said, his arms crossed before him. "So let me handle the magic, and you can just, bat your eyelashes or whatever else you did to cheat your way into this race."

My mouth dropped open in outrage. "If you recall, I got into this race by saving the girl you abandoned! You know, the injured one you refused to help despite the fact that a crocodile was about to eat her?" And since when did I ever bat my eyelashes?

"She would have been fine," Orin said. "They would have sent someone for her if you hadn't interfered."

"Well, you can't leave me behind," I said. "Because we both have to make it to the end if you want your precious money."

"You don't have to remind me," he snapped. "So like I said. Just let me handle the magic and stay the hell out of the way."

I huffed and turned towards the window, fury searing me. Who the hell did he think he was? I turned back to him. "I'll have you know I excelled in the physical and weapons training. You're *lucky* to have me as a partner."

"Says the girl at the bottom of the rankings."

"Says the faerie who was chosen last, and wouldn't have been chosen at all if I had anything to say about it! I'd rather go into Faerwild with Patricia in her stupid stilettos than you!" I screeched.

I heard snickers from the other competitors, and my face

burned. We were imploding, and we hadn't even gone over the Hedge.

"Just stay out of my way," he said, pinning me with his dark gaze. "I won't let you hold me back."

Orin and I said nothing else to each other the rest of the day. Not when we were shuffled off the bus into a forbidding forest, not when we lined up in a semi-circle around a pair of tall, weathered standing stones carved with squiggles and slashes. Patricia appeared, looking fetching in what looked like tight riding pants, an emerald blazer, and knee-high chestnut boots. Apparently, this was her "forest" attire.

"It's the moment we've all been waiting for," she said to the camera. "Our contestants will be going over the Hedge, the human competitors for the first time. They don't know what they'll find. The dangers that will face them in Faerwild are real. Magical creatures unlike any they've ever seen. A landscape so foreign, it will put Wonderland to shame. They'll have to rely on the wisdom and cunning of their faerie partners to help them navigate challenges no human has ever faced. How well these partners work together will determine the fate of the race. And maybe their very lives."

Great. I wanted to cry. Or kick Orin. Or both. I was totally screwed. Across the circle from us stood the producers, the Faerie King, and a pack of cameramen with high-tech body rigs. I spotted Ben among them, and we locked eyes. He gave me an encouraging thumbs up, and I felt one tiny bit better. At least I'd have one friend in here.

"Each contestant will receive a backpack of items they'll need for the race. Also in the backpack is a clue that will help get them to the first checkpoint. This first trial of the race, the Sorcery Trial has three legs ending in three checkpoints—whoever reaches the last checkpoint first wins the Trial and will have a leg-up going into the second trial."

Patricia was milking this for all she was worth. "My handsome assistant will be passing out rings to each contestant." A good-looking man in a suit did just that, giving each of us a plain silver band. I held it in my hand, feeling its weight before I slipped it on my middle finger. "These are tracking devices that will enable us to know where you are at all times. There is a button on the inside that will signal us to evacuate you. But mark my words, do not choose evacuation lightly. Once you press that button, you're disqualified. You're out of the race, and that means your teammate is too." Okay, so do not press the button. I wouldn't be eliminating myself. Not after busting my ass to get here.

"Lastly, a cameraman or woman has been assigned to each team. They will join you now."

The five camera guys (and one girl) crossed around the circle, coming to stand with each of our teams. My heart soared when Ben stepped in between Orin and me. I grinned at him. Thank god for a friendly face.

"You are not allowed to seek aid from your camera crew. They have been supplied with a means of protection, shelter, and transport. These do not apply to you. If you utilize them, you are disqualified." Great. So Ben would be munching on popcorn on his portable couch while I ate magic crickets in the rain.

"The world will be watching your race, and you would do well to remember that," Patricia said, waving her hand wide. "Good luck to each of you."

My stomach flipped as she stepped back and the Faerie King stepped forward. He had changed into medieval garb, perhaps three-piece suits weren't the rage over the Hedge. He drew a line through the air and murmured under his breath, and a lavender glow winked to life between the two stones. The hair on the back of my neck rose with the energy emanating from it—I could feel the faint crackle of magic.

The king stepped back with a predatory smile. "Welcome to Faerwild, racers."

I licked my dry lips. This was it. I was going in.

11

I'd expected some kind of magic portal where I'd walk through a wall of light into another world. What I hadn't imagined was that before we were allowed into Faerwild, we'd all be lined up and sent through a metal detector similar to the ones I'd had to walk through at the airport. As with everything else so far, I was placed at the very back.

I watched as the competitors were taken one by one through a machine that turned out to be a full body scanner with a small screen attached to it, which an FFR employee was glued to. What were they looking for? We were all wearing the Lycra uniforms we'd been assigned, and there was hardly any room in them to hide anything. All our personal belongings had been left in safes back at Hennington House.

As each person passed through they were given a full body pat down at the other side for good measure and then walked over to the actual magical portal. By the time they got to me, I could see that the FFR guards, or whoever they'd hired to do security, were on edge as though they expected to find something.

The only one they'd pulled to one side was Ario, and that was because he'd stashed some chewing gum which they'd confiscated and thrown in a basket at the side of the scanning machine. I walked up to the scanner and stepped inside, adopting the position I'd seen the others take with my legs a foot apart and my hands crossed above my head. Although I couldn't see the screen, I could certainly see the three men and two women crowded round it, looks of concern and concentration on their faces as the large machine whirred around me.

"Step off the scanner and stand to one side, please," one of the women said, walking over to me with what looked like a paddle. "This is the same as you'd expect to find in any airport," she explained, pulling my arms out to the sides. "I'll pat you down, check for illegal substances and then my colleague will check you for any illegal magic."

I nodded, knowing they wouldn't find any of that on me. I couldn't even muster up any legal magic, let alone the illegal kind. As she ran the paddle up and down my legs, I wondered what exactly constituted illegal magic.

Once she was satisfied, a second woman walked over and placed her hands on my shoulders.

"This won't hurt, but you may feel a tingle. It's completely harmless and will let me know if you've got any magic you shouldn't have. I'm a detector and am fully trained, so there is nothing to worry about. Just stay completely still for me for a moment." I nodded to tell her that I understood and closed my eyes as her magic washed over me. As she had said, I felt a light vibration pass through my body.

"No metal, no drugs, no bombs. She's clean." I heard someone whisper.

Opening my eyes, I saw the first woman chatting discretely to the head guard who nodded his head. Not quite discretely enough though, because I caught every word. Something about the magic running through me had made my senses keener, and though the guards were whispering, I could hear them perfectly.

No bombs? They actually thought one of us might try to take explosives into the faerie realm? Why would they think that?

"You're done," the second woman said before turning and giving the head guard a thumbs up. Finally, I was allowed to join my fellow contestants in front of the portal that would take us into Faerwild.

The magic field enveloped me as I walked through the wall of lilac light next to Orin. As we were the last to go through, I heard Patricia speaking to the cameras just before the magic cut off any sound from the human world.

"Caerleon isn't the only portal from the human world to the faerie world, but don't come here thinking you can get through. Once all our competitors are through, the Faerie King will seal the portal, and there will be no way in or out. Other places that have enough energy to create portals include Stonehenge in England; Pammukale in Turkey; Fingal's Cave in Scotland; Havasupai in Arizo..." I couldn't hear any more as the magic blocked out any noise.

As my vision cleared, the landscape before me presented itself. Directly in front of me stood my fellow contestants and the Faerie king, not to mention the camera people. To the right, in the distance, across a sparkling stretch of water, a huge city dominated the horizon. Soaring spires and towers, unlike anything I'd seen before, sprouted from the ground between smaller buildings and trees.

Hope bloomed in me. I knew in my heart, that's where Cass was. It would be easy to hide someone inside a sprawling magical metropolis. And more importantly, it would be easy to get lost in.

I'd not heard her voice in over three years, but I swore I heard her call my name. I jumped, trying to see where it came from, but it was only an old jackdaw cawing in the tree above. I'd been in Faerwild all of thirty seconds, and already, the hair on my arms was standing to attention, and my thoughts were on Cass. Not that I had thought it would be any different, but now that I was here, it was as though I could feel her. I closed my eyes to try to get a grip on the feeling, but the only thing I noticed was that the weird crackling of the faeries' magic had ceased. I could no longer feel it, probably because everywhere in Faerwild was magic and so it all blended together. My endless headache from the past month was also beginning to clear. Well, that was something. It would suck to go through this entire trial with a migraine.

I opened my eyes and focused my attention back on the contestants in front of me. All eyes—human and fae alike— were turned to a huge shimmering wall that seemed to go on for miles in both directions and the gate that was opening to let us all in. This was my chance. I could find Cass without the king's boon, without all the danger and rigmarole. I needed to slip away before anyone noticed I was gone. My muscles bunched to move when I felt the cold grip of someone's hand on my wrist.

"Don't get any ideas about going in there ahead of me," Orin said, his voice low. He'd misunderstood my intentions and thought I was going to cheat him. What a joke.

I wrestled my wrist away and shot him my best dirty look.

The other competitors had already passed through the gate, and all eyes were on Orin and me. My heart sank, and I kicked myself for my hesitation. I'd missed my chance. I'd actually have to go through the gate and compete in the race.

Without waiting for Orin, I tightened the straps on my backpack and stalked through the gates.

With a crackling boom, the magical force field closed behind us, leaving us at the very edge of a dark forest. The canopy of trees cut out most of the light, leaving me on edge. I could feel the magic here, its presence crawling over my awareness. That, compounded with the eerie silence, was doing nothing for my nerves.

Ben kept his red-blinking camera trained on me as I surveyed my surroundings, struggling to keep the rising panic off my face and the thought of Cass from my mind. She'd been brought here against her will. I was sure of that now. The dreams of her being taken by the fae had gotten stronger over the past month, though I was yet to see the faerie's face. I always woke before he completely turned to face me. I wondered if this was the same view Cass had seen when she first came to Faerwild. Was she as intimidated by it as I felt? Had she been terrified? Was she still?

At least, most of the other competitors looked equally unnerved by the strange silence and faint crackle of magic, standing stiffly, heads swiveling around.

Duncan and Yael wasted no time and broke into a run, heading into the woods. Within a moment, the dark shadows of the forest swallowed them up, and it was like they'd never passed by.

I pulled my face into what I hoped looked like an expression of excitement rather than fear and took a step forward.

"There will be traps out there," I heard Dulcina whisper to her partner, Phillip. "I think we should hang back and let the others get caught up in them first."

I watched as Phillip rolled his eyes. "That would have been a good plan if you didn't have the voice of a foghorn."

She looked embarrassed as she realized everyone had heard what she'd said. "I'm sorry. I didn't mean..."

"It's fine," huffed Orin. "We're competitors. If someone else gets slowed down by a trap, I'm not going to waste any tears."

Dulcina's cheeks reddened, offsetting her purple locks.

I stepped forward. "I think what Orin means is that it might be wise to stick together for a bit while we get used to our new surroundings."

I saw a few others nod their heads which told me that I wasn't the only one feeling nervous.

Goth girl and sexy incubus (I really needed to start calling them by their real names...Molly and Ario) took the lead with the rest of us trailing behind. As I stepped deeper into the woods to follow them, Orin hissed in my ear. "That's not what I meant at all. I'm not following these idiots for long. I don't know about you, but I came here to win. That means leaving everyone else in the dust, including you if you can't keep up."

I opened my mouth in shock as he stalked off in front of me. Great. As if I didn't have enough to worry about, my own partner was just as willing to work against me as with me. It was with this thought in my mind that I stepped into the inky blackness of the woods in the footsteps of my fellow competitors.

~

THE TENSION of the first moments over the Hedge faded as we continued into the woods and nothing untoward happened beyond Phillip tripping and scraping his knee.

As we walked, I checked out the contents of my backpack. I had a knife, some string, a pair of binoculars and a water canteen that was unfortunately empty. I also had a thick cream envelope, sealed shut with a wax seal. The seal of the Obanstones. It was the first clue. Pushing it to one side, I scrabbled about in the rest of the backpack, hoping to find some food, but that was it. We were going to have to hunt and forage for food ourselves.

The hours passed, and we'd done nothing but walk. I could picture John's face as we cut through the darkness. This didn't make great TV at all.

The cloying darkness and quietness of the woods made me feel more uneasy with each step. Something was going to happen soon, I could feel it. They wouldn't let the first episode go to air without something dramatic happening.

I was just about to voice my opinion to Molly when I heard a scream up ahead. My heart began to hammer in my chest, but I was ready. I pulled the knife out from my belt where I'd fastened it, and held it out, ready for whatever was going to come my way. The darkness of night had settled over us like a heavy blanket; I couldn't see who it was that had screamed. Whoever it was, they needed help.

Without considering the repercussions, I ran forward past Molly, Orin, and Ario.

The scream rang out again as I pelted through the darkness towards the sound. I skidded to a stop as I reached the source.

It was Sophie. I found her struggling against a large

mass of whipping vines that were entwining themselves around her wrist and legs.

Tristam was beside her, throwing purple light unsuccessfully at the vines.

The more she tried twisting and turning her body, the tighter the vines became.

The panic in Tristam's face was apparent as his magic had no effect at all. Purple light bounced off the vines in all directions, causing me to duck, so I didn't inadvertently get hit.

"Stop!" I yelled.

Tristam looked my way, and the purple light stopped.

"What are you doing?" screamed Sophia. "She's on another team. She wants me dead." Tears streamed down her face, and her voice was hoarse with the effort of screaming.

Tristam looked at me uncertainly as I shook my head.

I held up my knife and lunged at her. From behind me, someone else screamed, and a flash of blue light hit me in the side, sending me careening forward right into Sophia and causing pain, unlike nothing I'd felt before.

She spit right in my face as I lifted the dagger towards her.

"Kill me if you want, but Tristam would never go for the likes of you."

Another flash of blue light and the pain in my side was joined by a pain in my left leg.

I bought the knife down on the nearest vine and blood spurted everywhere, covering both Sophia and me, and yet I still hacked away, despite the shock on her face.

The vines were not a plant at all, but some kind of living breathing monster in disguise. As I hacked off limb after limb of the disgusting green beast, Sophia finally realized I was trying to save her, not kill her, and pulled against the limbs.

The searing pain in my back and leg burned white hot, but I didn't stop until Sophia fell forward and the beast was dead. I collapsed to the ground beside Sophia.

"What happened?" Tristam asked.

Sophia grabbed hold of him and sobbed into his shirt, smearing it with the monster's blood. It was like a scene from a horror movie. In the corner of my eye, I saw Ben and another cameraman filming everything.

I should have stood up and acted all heroic for the public, but my entire being burned like I was on fire and I couldn't move.

"I'm so sorry!" I heard a small voice say. I recognized it as Zee's high-pitched singsong voice. "I thought you were trying to kill Sophia."

I felt a hand on my back, and for a second, it felt like my skin had peeled right off, but then sweet relief set in as the pain was sucked out of me. Seconds later, I felt the same thing on my leg.

I took a deep breath and sat up. Zee gazed down at me with concern in her eyes, her mouth open slightly, displaying two curved canines, like a vampire. The tattoos on her face glowed faintly with the afterglow of the magic she had used.

"I wouldn't have hurt you if I'd known you were trying to help. I just thought..." She trailed off. She'd always seemed so tough during the training, so it was a surprise to see tears welling in the corners of her eyes.

"It was an accident," I said, reassuring her.

She gave me a shy smile as she helped me up off the ground.

"There's a tower in a clearing up ahead," Phillip pointed

out. "I think we've all had enough excitement for one day. Let's camp there."

I'd not realized how exhausted I was, but as I stood on shaky legs, the idea of settling down for the night consumed me.

I let the others walk ahead and followed them to the tower Phillip had mentioned, my feet dragging. The tower was an ominous looking place with some freakishly large birds circling the top of it.

"I'll get us some food," Zee said, eager to make up for what she'd done to me.

"And I'll start the fire," added Tristam. He waved his hands, and a flame erupted from the ground. All around me, people were catching small animals and finding berries to eat, leaving me feeling useless.

I sat down next to Tristam, mainly to keep warm next to his fire. At least, that's what I told myself I was doing. My ass had barely touched the leaf-covered floor when Sophia sidled up to me.

"Can I have a word with you?" she asked. She shot a warm smile at Tristam as I stood.

I followed her to the opposite side of the tower. From here, I could barely hear the others, and the flames of Tristam's fire didn't shed enough light for me to see her all that well.

A flutter of nerves flooded through me as I wondered what she had in store for me. I'd thought she wanted to thank me for saving her, but now that we were out of sight of everyone else, I wasn't so sure. She could murder me in a second and tell the others a beast had taken me. Though Ben and his camera were watching.

I was struck by the fact that out here, far from the reach of the studio executives or even the Faerie King, it was every man, woman, and faerie for themselves. Patricia and Gabe and the others had warned us that the dangers over the Hedge would be real, but still. I hadn't been prepared. No one had stepped in to save Sophia, other than me, that was. No one stopped Zee when she'd injured me. No producer jumped out of the bushes and called a time out.

Of course, they didn't, I schooled myself. They wanted ratings, and so that meant the bloodier, the better. Sophia was covered in the stuff. I could still see it glistening in the low light. With a start, I realized that I must be covered in it too.

I moved my hand up to my face where I'd felt some of the splatter and wiped my sleeve across it. When I pulled my arm back, I could see the dark reddish brown of the monster's blood.

"Don't worry," Sophia remarked, seeing the dismay on my face. "I'm sure Tristam will help take the blood out of our clothes. It's only a little spell. I'd do it myself, but I'm still tired from fighting the monster, and you can't can you?"

I listened to her words carefully. She sounded like she was being nice and sincere, but already she was asking me if I truly belonged in here. She was sniffing for information. It seemed that saving her hadn't made us friends. Not that I was surprised.

"I'm tired too," I said, affecting a yawn to add weight to my argument.

"Ah, well," she singsonged. "I just wanted to thank you. I'm sure Tristam will too. He was just telling me earlier how glad he was to have me as a partner, and I wouldn't want him to lose me. I think we'll be good friends by the end of this."

My dislike of the woman slid into the loathe category at

her false words. I sputtered out a *you're welcome* and headed back to camp.

The others had caught a couple of those weird birds and were busy roasting them over the fire. I sat back, not wanting to talk to the others, and listened to Phillip telling the rest of the contestants that there was no door to the tower. Apparently, he'd walked around the whole thing. Strange, I'd been around the other side and I'd not seen him. Not that I'd seen a door either. The grey stone tower was nothing but a marker, but something about it gave me the creeps.

Talking of giving me the creeps, Orin sat down beside me and handed me a bit of the cooked bird.

"It's not poisoned," he said when he caught me looking at it suspiciously. I wouldn't put it past him to kill me off. The list of people I didn't trust was growing at a rapid rate, and I'd only been over the Hedge for a few hours.

I took a bite and chewed thoughtfully on the cooked meat. It was good. Better than I'd expected it to be.

"What did Sophia want?" Orin whispered.

I looked over at her. Her face was lit up from the glow of the campfire. As I watched, she laughed at something Tristam said and ran her hand down his leg. I noticed that she no longer had any blood on her. Tristam must have performed the spell, after all. He'd just forgotten to do it on me.

Never mind. A bit of blood on me would make me look fearless. I leaned in towards Orin and whispered back at him. "She wanted to be my friend."

He huffed beside me. "I don't trust her. She's no friend of yours."

As I looked back at her, she caught my eye and smiled through pursed lips. It was not a friendly smile.

I shook my head blackly. "I can't believe I'm saying this, but I think you might be right."

Orin raised an eyebrow. "Do tell?"

How could I tell him that I thought Sophia might be jealous of me? Ok, not jealous as such, but she must have seen Tristam and I talking back in Wales. Plus, she never took her eyes off him for more than a millisecond, so it was conceivable that she'd seen him use his magic to knock the apple from his father's hand in the trial.

"She's a bitch," was what I actually said.

Orin nodded and conjured up a sleeping bag which he slithered into. His velvet voice was low as he leaned in to whisper to me. "We set off when everyone else is asleep. Get a jump on the competition. I don't trust anyone else. Duncan and Yael had the right idea by going off alone."

"Fine," I conceded. I didn't trust half the contestants either. Not that I trusted Orin, but I was stuck with him. I trusted him to, at least, try to keep me alive. He needed me to get past the checkpoints with him, or he'd be disqualified.

I pulled my knees close to me as the temperature dropped, tucking my frigid fingers into my armpits. How gentlemanly of Orin to offer to conjure *me* a sleeping bag. He probably expected me to keep guard over him. I snorted at the thought.

Well, there was only one person I'd be keeping guard for. And that person was me.

Someone kicked me awake just before dawn. I cried out in disorientation, and a cold hand slapped over my mouth.

"Quiet," someone hissed in my ear.

I struggled to turn and saw Orin's dark eyes. I relaxed slightly and raised my eyebrows.

He removed his hand from my face. "Everyone's still asleep. Let's go."

I nodded. It's not like I had a cozy sleeping bag to cuddle up in.

I got to my feet and found I was stiff with cold with a crick in my neck and dried blood covering me. I probably looked like a wild animal.

"Let's go," Orin repeated with some urgency. I turned, and a blinking red light greeted me. I squinted and saw Ben's curly head peek out from behind the camera. He waved. It seemed it would be the three of us.

I followed Orin, and Ben followed me through the trees silent as a sentinel. I could just see through the watery gray light of dawn, but still, my feet seemed to find every root and stray branch.

Orin walked before me like a lord of the forest, his FFR uniform neat, his dark hair combed. I glowered at his back. Whatever grooming magic he had, would it hurt him to share it with his partner?

I trudged behind him, and Ben sped up until he was walking beside me. I felt a nudge in my side, and I looked down to find a protein bar being waggled at me. An illicit protein bar! The camera crew wasn't supposed to share their food with us. But…my stomach rumbled. If Orin and Ben were both walking in front of me, there was no one to see my transgression.

I snatched the bar from him and opened it as stealthily as possible. It tasted amazing. It was the best thing that had happened to me in the last twenty-four hours. I wanted to spring at give Ben and give him a hug.

Orin came to a stop before me at the shore of a tinkling stream. He pulled off his backpack and retrieved his canteen. "We should fill up."

"It's safe?" I asked. After the weird vine monster, I wasn't taking anything for granted. For all I knew, this river was going to morph into a tsunami and sweep me out to shore.

He nodded. "Rivers are usually home to water nymphs. They can be mischievous but likely won't cause permanent harm. You want to stay away from lakes, as they're more likely to be a habitat for water horses."

"Water horses?" I said as I leaned down to lay my canteen into the water. "Like the ones Liv Tyler conjured in Lord of the Rings?"

Orin blinked at me like I was a complete moron. "No. Like the kind that pull you into the water and eat the flesh from your bones."

I froze, my mouth aghast. "Oh."

"This isn't Hollywood anymore. You should assume everything in faerie wants to eat you or kill you."

"Are you included in that?" I countered.

"Depends on if you slow me down. Keep up, and we'll be fine."

I sat my full canteen on a bed of pine needles on the riverbank and plunged my arms into the frigid water. I scrubbed my arms and my face, letting the monster's blood color the clear water.

Dawn had broken, and birds chirped on nearby branches. It was almost like camping back home. If you ignored Orin's tipped ears. And that glowing purple cluster of flowers. And the monster blood I was rinsing off.

"I think I've figured out the first clue," Orin said, pulling out the envelope that had been placed in each of our backpacks. The clue to the first checkpoint. I hadn't even looked at it yesterday; I'd been so set on (a) not dying, and (b) collapsing into a freezing uncomfortable sleep on the rocky forest floor.

"What's the clue?" I asked, doing my best to wipe my face dry with my jacket.

"It's a poem," Orin said.

WHO'S RIDING SO LATE *through th' endless wild?*
The father 'It is with his infant child.
He thinks the boy's well off in his arm,
He grasps him tightly, he keeps him warm.

ORIN RECITED the verse with a lilting tone that sent a shiver up my spine. For a moment, he wasn't the cruel black faerie who might stab me in the back, but a boy—reading words from a book that filled him with reverence.

He looked up and met my rapt gaze. I jerked my eyes away, embarrassed to be caught staring. I cleared my throat. "I don't know what the heck that means."

"It's a poem. A human poem," he said as if that explained it. "By Goethe? Erlkönig?" he said, incredulous.

I shook my head. "You might as well be speaking Greek."

"German," he said.

"Okay?" I replied, annoyed. Whatever.

He heaved a longsuffering sigh. "It's a poem by a German poet named Von Goethe. It's about the Erl-King. He's a famous faerie, lord of the forest."

"Awesome," I said, still not getting what Orin was going on about.

"Gods, what do they teach you humans in school?" Orin said. "The Erl-King is a legend in the human world, too. But he's a real faerie. Ancient. He is the ruler of this forest. His castle is nearby..."

My eyes grew wide. "Ohhhhhh! You think that's the first checkpoint?"

"Houston, we have takeoff."

"That's not the saying," I said, grateful to know some-thing. "It's 'Houston, we have a problem.'"

"Same difference," Orin scoffed, shoving his canteen back into his pack and shouldering it.

"So...where is this Erl-King's house?" I asked.

"I'm...not exactly sure," Orin admitted. "He's notoriously reclusive. You don't really find him unless he wants you to."

"Oh!" I crossed my arms over my chest. "Looks like Mister Smarty-pants doesn't have it all figured out."

"Mister Smarty-pants?" he said. "Is that some crude human moniker?"

"Yes," I admitted frostily. "Though your nickname is actually Mr. Crabbypants."

"And yours is Thorn in my Side," he scoffed, taking a step towards me.

"Trust me, I want to be in nothing of *yours*," I said, squaring my shoulders and facing him. Except maybe his sleeping bag, and then only because it looked so damn cozy.

All of a sudden, fury overtook me. Who did this asshole think he was? He was supposed to be the one person I could count on in this mad place, and instead, he treated me with nothing but contempt.

I shook my head. "You were the last person I ever would have wanted to partner up with—"

"At least we can agree on that," he interrupted.

"But," I said, ignoring the sting of his comment, "We're stuck with each other. So don't you think we should at least try to get along? Work together?"

"From what I see, you don't have anything to offer this team. So yes, I will drag your dead weight behind me through this competition, because I *have to* in order to win it. But I don't see much point in trying to work together. The clue was obviously tailored to the human partner as Von Goethe is human, but you didn't even know that."

I recoiled at his words, my mouth opening and closing. The *nerve* of this faerie... "How dare you..." I managed, but I was devoid of witty comebacks as my thoughts flew from my head. No one told me I'd have to be well versed in poetry. It was hardly the first thing anyone would expect to have to know in a race like this.

As we looked at each other furiously, I suddenly became aware of Ben's blinking red light, just feet from the two of us, taking it all in. I huffed and broke off, turning from Orin.

Tears prickled at the corners of my eyes and I didn't want Orin to see them, let alone the rest of the world.

"Do you, at least, know a general direction?" I asked thickly.

"I think...that way." He pointed.

"You think?" I said, my voice rising. "I guess I'm not the only dead weight on this team." I knew the comment wasn't entirely fair to him since I hadn't even figured out the riddle, and definitely didn't know which direction to head. But he was pissing me off something fierce! So I kept talking. "How are we supposed to find the Erl-King if you don't even know what direction to head?"

"We might be able to help with that," a sinuous voice said behind me.

13

I turned sharply.

Ben did the same, almost dropping his camera in the process.

Two staggeringly beautiful women, way too short to be human, stared up at me, their eyes bright with narrow green irises circling the largest pupils I'd ever seen. Those huge eyes put me at ease, the same reaction my body and brain might have to a crateful of puppies. These were no puppies, though. They were...

"Nymphs!" Orin spat out in disgust.

Okay, well, at least I knew what they were now. Standing at about equal height to my waist wearing clothes that looked to be made out of leaves, the two miniature women smiled up at me warmly.

"We know where the Erl-King lives," they chorused, their two voices in perfect simpatico. The one on the right nodded her bouncy blonde curls as the other one, who had waist-long, dark hair, pointed out into the distance.

I followed her finger with my eyes. All I could see were

trees, but that was nothing new. I'd seen nothing but trees for hours.

"Is it in the forest?" I asked them.

The blonde one nodded again and giggled. Her tinkling laugh made me almost want to join in.

I noticed Orin scowling out of the corner of my eye. They obviously didn't have the same effect on him as they were having on me. Maybe faeries were immune to nymph magic? Or maybe Orin was immune to giggling. It certainly seemed that way, the joyless oaf.

I picked up the backpack I'd dropped to the ground and gestured to the nymphs to lead the way. The pair of them held hands and danced ahead, stopping only when they realized we weren't following.

Orin stared at me like I had a second head. "What do you think you're doing? You aren't actually going to follow them are you?"

I shrugged. "Look around. We're in the middle of nowhere. We have nothing else to go on. So why not?"

Orin rolled his eyes at me. "I'll tell you why not. We're in the middle of a race. A race designed by people who want to see action at all costs. Do you think they are going to send pretty little creatures to take us exactly where we need to go or do you think they might send cute nymphs to lure us into danger? Which scenario do you think makes for better viewing?"

I had to admit he had a point. The only action, so far, had been Sophia getting caught up in the vine monster. I knew John would want to see more of the same. Still...I glanced back at the nymphs. They were ballroom dancing while waiting for us. Both had their eyes closed and wide smiles on their faces as they twirled each other around to the sound of their own music. Even my cold dead heart was lifted at the sight of it.

I shrugged my shoulders and took a step towards them, calling to Orin over my shoulder. "Suit yourself, but I'm going to follow them." Even if he was right, we had no leads to the location of the Erl-King's house. No leads but them.

I had to stifle a smile as I heard a muttered string of expletives followed by the sound of Orin's footfalls behind me. Not that he really had a choice in the matter. Not if he wanted to win. He could bicker with me and call me dead weight as much as he liked, but he still had to cross the finish line with me to be crowned the winner. Thinking that way made me feel a little more powerful. The guy might act like he wanted me dead half the time; but if push came to shove, he'd have to save me. Without me, there was literally no point to him participating in this damn race at all. I decided to hold on to the thought for when things got bad because let's face it; we'd had it easy so far.

Despite my apparent trust of the two nymphs, I did take to heart what Orin had said. As I followed them through the darkness of the woods, I was careful only to tread where they had trod and to keep an eye out for any traps.

They kept a few paces ahead, singing a pretty little tune in harmony. Orin made sure to stay behind me.

Ben had disappeared completely, but I knew that didn't mean we weren't being filmed, it just meant that he was probably wearing some kind of magic cloaking device. We'd been told that most of the time we'd not see our cameramen and women. The execs had told us it was because they didn't want to ruin the ambiance for us or distract us, but I knew the real reason—it was so we would forget we were on TV at all. If the cameras were in our faces all the time, we'd all be guarded, but if we couldn't see them, we'd do and say things that we wouldn't normally let ourselves do in front of fifty million people.

I felt my stomach rumble again, realizing I'd eaten nothing but Ben's illicit protein bar since morning.

"Can we stop? I'm hungry."

I'd wanted Orin to say it first, but after a few hours of hunger pains, I was willing to look like the weaker of the two of us.

The nymphs scattered, both heading quickly in different directions into the woods. I'd barely had time to register where they'd taken off to when they came back with handfuls of berries that they offered up to me. The berries were plump and glistening, and I could honestly say I'd never seen anything that looked so delicious in my life. I reached out to grab one when Orin bounded forward, knocking the berries all over the floor. "Those are bellow berries."

"What?" I turned to glare at him while the two nymphs giggled behind me. I'd never heard of bellow berries before.

"Eat one of those and your insides will liquefy, before turning to gas and within ten minutes your abdomen will literally explode."

I surveyed the berries scattered all over the ground with new horror.

"I told you not to trust them!" He kicked out, aiming for the nymphs, but they were too fast for him. They ran just out of sight into the woods with Orin in pursuit.

I hesitantly followed him, knowing it worked both ways. He was stuck with me, but I was also stuck with his sorry ass. I'd barely run more than twenty feet when I crashed right into him, almost sending the pair of us toppling over the edge of a cliff.

"Watch it!"

I took a step back, my heart pounding at the steep drop right in front of us.

"Sorry. I guess you were right. I shouldn't have trusted those nymphs." I could hear them giggling from somewhere above me, but they were hidden out of sight in the leaves above us.

"Actually, you were right to trust them. Look."

I turned my attention from the branches above my head and looked out. We were right at the very edge of the forest, and below us, stretching out for miles, was the most incredible view.

"We can see the entire playing field from here," I murmured, taking in a deep breath and mentally plotting a route. The magical walls that surrounded us shimmered faintly in the distance, showing me the scope of what we were dealing with. My eyes flicked to the right and spotted the large city I'd seen when I'd first arrived in the faerie realm. My heart squeezed painfully, thinking of Cass. She was somewhere in that city, I was sure of it. Orin pointed out a castle a mile ahead and I nodded. It looked as good a place as any to head next, and was hopefully the Erl-King's lair.

Orin was going painfully slowly down the rocky path, but even with the great deliberation he was giving each step, he still managed to trip. I dashed forward and caught hold of his bag, holding it tight to stop him falling right over the edge.

"Maybe I should go first here, and you can follow my path," I said, pulling him back against the cliff face.

Climbing was easy for me. Dad used to say I was part mountain goat. I might not be able to do much in this place, but I knew my strengths, and this was one.

"I think that would be a prudent decision."

Wow, the guy was actually agreeing with me. Getting

him to agree was one thing, passing him on the insanely thin path was another. He pulled his bag from his back to enable him to push his body straight to the cliff face.

Even sucking in, I still had to hold onto him as I sidled past, lest I fall to my death over the edge. Slowly, I edged past him. Feeling his body pressed against mine was a strange sensation. I'd spent the last twenty-four hours wanting to be as far away from him as possible, and now we were as close as we could possibly get. It would be easy for him to push me over the edge right now. He wouldn't even have to use his hands. He could literally breathe out quickly, and I'd be freefalling. I glanced up at him, wondering if he'd had the same thought, but his eyes were wide, filled with terror.

"You're scared of heights!" I marveled.

"Just hurry up," he hissed through gritted teeth.

I edged past him quickly, a smug feeling taking up space in my chest. There was no doubt in my mind he was scared of heights. The cocky bastard had finally shown his true feelings about something. The only thing that confused me was the fact that he'd been safely backed against the cliff face. I was the one with all the risk. Had he actually been worried that I would fall? Now that was a confusing thought.

The path widened slightly, and some of the tension left me. The terrain was still difficult going, but at least, the chances of falling to our deaths were significantly reduced.

Once at the bottom, it was a short walk to the strange castle. I'd not noticed from so far away, but the four towers that made up each corner were covered entirely in vines and leaves. It was as if the castle were a living thing.

I opened my mouth to say as such when I felt something touch my arm. Swiveling around, I saw it was only Orin.

"Thank you... for helping me back there."

My already open mouth widened in shock. Orin had actually thanked me. "Maybe you walked through a spell on the way down. You're not acting like yourself."

He gave me a brief smile, shocking me further still. "Very funny," he replied, going back to the Orin I knew. "Maybe instead of wasting it on snark, you could put your brainpower to work figuring out how the hell we're going to get inside?"

I made a face at him. But as I looked at the castle once again, I wasn't sure my brainpower would be enough.

14

As we walked closer to the huge castle, the sound of music reached our ears. Music and...merry-making. Laughter and voices drifted over the walls towards us.

"Maybe he's having a party?" I suggested, half-joking.

"He probably is," Orin replied matter-of-factly. "Faeries are notorious for their revelry and debauchery. Their parties last for days...weeks."

"Do you think we could get ourselves invited somehow?"

Orin looked at me appraisingly, then looked back at Ben, who had materialized with his blinking red camera. "Humans are enough of a novelty in Faerwild that your presence here might warrant an invite in."

I narrowed my eyes. "Why do I suddenly feel like bait?"

"Once you're in, wriggle off the hook and find the clue at the next checkpoint," Orin said with a wide smile that didn't reach his eyes.

I scowled.

We rounded the corner and approached the front gate.

"Jacq," Orin said, turning suddenly and grabbing my

upper arm. He loomed in my vision, tall and imposing and so very fae. "Don't touch anything. What I said about the forest applies double to this castle. It's dangerous." Then he spun and stalked towards the gate.

"Aww," I called after him. "I could almost believe you care."

The guard at the gate was a well-muscled faerie of a type I had never seen. Satyr perhaps, if I remembered from the Greek history unit in my World Civilization class. He had little pricked horns poking from his curly hair, and his feet tapered to cloven hooves and legs covered in wiry hair. He would almost look friendly, but for the wickedly sharp lance clutched in his gloved hand.

"Name," he asked monotonously.

"Orin Treebaum and Jacqueline Cunningham," Orin said smoothly. "We're Faerie Race contestants. The Erl-King has invited us to the gathering."

Huh. I didn't realize he knew my full name. A parchment scroll materialized in the guard's other hand, and he scanned down it.

My stomach flipped, and I braced myself for the spear to be leveled at us. My mind already raced for an alternate solution to gain entry. Scale the wall? We had some rope in our packs, but no grappling hook...maybe climb a tree?

"Enjoy the party," the goat-faerie said, snapping the scroll shut and stepping aside.

I struggled to keep the shock off my face and paste a look of entitlement there instead. Maybe all of the contestants were on the guest list.

The inside of the Erl-King's castle was the most extraordinary of the strange and wonderful sights I'd seen since crossing over the Hedge. It was like being inside a huge living tree. The walls were crowned with ivy vines and foliage; other walls made of undulating wood somehow magically formed around doorways and windows. Furniture was carved wood as well as if the craftsman simply sang the wood into form. Not a joint or nail was visible anywhere. My dad, who fancied himself an amateur woodworker, would kill to get a look at this. Hanging from the ceiling high above us were lanterns lit by some sort of faerie glow, a soft white light that lent the space a faerie tale feel. It was extraordinary.

As we passed from room to room, our boots muffled on the packed dirt floor, I finally quit gawking and turned to the task at hand.

Orin had a look on his face that was even more grumpy than normal.

"What's your problem?" I asked.

"It feels wrong," he said. "Why did they let us in so easily? Suddenly, I feel like I'm wriggling on the hook too."

"Welcome to the club, chum. Maybe the hard part was breaking the riddle..." but even as I said it, I knew that sentiment was foolishly optimistic. They'd make each part of getting to this checkpoint difficult if they could.

"Let's just be careful," I amended.

A wide arching set of doors yawned before us, light spilling out from the room beyond together with a jaunty tune of fiddle and flute.

I blinked at the brightness and the splendor as we passed into the room for before me, were dozens of fancifully clad faeries of all shapes and sizes. And, my eyes and my empty stomach couldn't help but notice the room also contained an impossibly long table laden with every type of food imaginable. Across the far wall, doors opened out into the night where more faeries danced and reveled around a giant bonfire.

My stomach yowled in protest, and I felt my feet towed towards the beautiful sight—little cakes glistening with honey and powdered sugar, juicy cuts of meat, golden-brown loaves of bread with little pads of salted butter. God, I wanted bread.

"Look!" Orin said excitedly, pointing to the front of the room.

My eyes followed his finger to a huge fireplace. Atop the mantle were six ornate stands. Four of the stands held beautiful golden apples.

"Six stands," he said. "Six teams. I bet the apples are the next clue!"

As soon as he said it, I knew it was so. "Two teams have already gotten here?" I said in dismay. Damn. I thought we were doing better than that.

"Well, we're still the third," Orin said.

I looked at him in shock. "Orin Treebaum...Was that..."—my hand drifted to my chest in surprise —"Optimism?"

Instantly his usual dark expression slammed back into place and I regretted my jest. "Let's grab it," I said.

We navigated around the side of the room, dangerously close to the food table. I reached out a hand and grabbed a golden chicken leg. I didn't know the next time I'd be able to eat.

We reached the mantle and Orin reached up and retrieved the apple. His movement was cautious as if he expected the whole room to transform around us Indiana Jones style as soon as the weight of the apple was gone from its resting place. But nothing happened. No one even looked our way.

I sighed and lifted the chicken leg to my mouth.

Orin's eyes went wide, and he batted it out of my hand

just inches from my teeth.

I watched it skitter across the floor in horror. "What the hell was that for!"

"I told you not to touch anything!" Orin said through gritted teeth. "That food is likely enchanted. If you want to end up like them,"—he pointed to the revelers around the bonfire—"dancing for an eternity until your feet fall off, be my guest. But I'd prefer to get the hell out of here and figure out our next clue."

I looked at the dancers around the fire with dismay, suddenly feeling sick to my very empty stomach. Dancing for eternity most certainly did not sound like something I would like to do. One of the dancers looked familiar, and I narrowed my eyes, squinting against the brightness of the fire.

Horror flooded me. The dancer *was* familiar! Her jet-black hair, her tanned skin—it was Genevieve!

Genevieve disappeared behind the bonfire, and another dancer came into view. One with red hair as bright as the flames behind her and purple tattoos on her face. Zee!

"Orin, it's Geneviee and Zee," I said. "They're dancing."

"Well, they must have been stupid enough to eat something," he said. "Let's go." He tried to tug me towards the door, but I dug in my heels. "We can't just leave them to dance until their feet fall off!"

"They're our competition, not your girlfriends," Orin countered. "We can, and we will."

"I should not be surprised you'd say that, after you abandoned that poor girl in the audition," I snapped. "But Genevieve was my sister's friend. I'm not leaving her." I pulled my arm out from his grip and launched myself across the room towards the open doors before Orin could move to stop me.

15

Getting to Genevieve wasn't as easy as I'd expected. Every time I got close, she waltzed off in another direction, or another enchanted dancer scooted between us.

The dancers whirled around me in a kaleidoscope of color and bodies. Now that I was up close, I could see the lines of pain etched into their faces. How long had they been dancing like this? The heat of the bonfire reminded me of the wall of flame at the auditions and in some ways, getting to Genevieve and Zee was similar to the obstacles I'd dodged back then. Just grasping at them was doing nothing. I needed a plan. Taking a step back, I assessed the situation.

There was a perfect symmetry to the dancing, a pattern. It took a few minutes to figure out as everyone changed partners so often, but it was definitely there.

"Time is ticking," growled Orin from over my shoulder. "And there's no way you'll get to them. Let's just go and pretend we never saw them."

"There's a way through," I muttered, ignoring Orin.

He opened his mouth to make what I'm sure was some

smart-ass retort, but his words were lost to me as I dove into the dancing throng, taking the arms of a male faerie who looked to be on the verge of tears. He seemed surprised to have a new partner, and for a second, his eyes lit up.

"It's nice to have a change," he sighed. "It's just a shame a pretty little thing like you got caught. I'm still hungry you know. So not worth it."

I was just about to take exception to him calling me a pretty little thing—for a start, I was a good foot taller than him—but the partners were changing again, and I found myself in the arms of a very tall and very ugly woman.

"I wouldn't mind," she said in a very gruff voice, "but if I'd known I'd be dancing, I'd have worn different shoes."

I gave her a lame smile, wondering where she found shoes her size. I also wondered how many times these people had started a conversation only to be sent spinning into another person's arms to start all over again. I was pretty sure what she'd just said to me was only half of the sentence. I opened my mouth to say something back to her when a spit of fire blasted past me with a screech. It was only when I turned my head that I realized it was Zee, but she had already disappeared back into the crowd.

Zee was not who I was aiming for. When I'd started watching for a pattern, Genevieve was the one I'd seen first, and it was her I was planning to get to. I'd worry about Zee afterward. Two more partner , and I was finally face-to-face with her. I had less than a minute to free her before she'd once again be thrust into another dancer's hands.

I grabbed hold of the top of each of her arms tightly and tried pulling her through the crowd.

"It won't work," Genevieve grimaced with the pain I was causing her. "You can't fight magic with force!"

Her words only made me more determined. "Just watch me."

I pulled harder, fighting with all my strength, but she carried on dancing in the same direction as the crowd.

A grimace wrinkled her face, and I realized, in my desperation to remove her from the dance floor, that I was hurting her.

I let go, and she disappeared back into the swarm of dancing faeries. My heart plummeted with disappointment, but I didn't have time to dwell on it as another dancer came at me hastily and carried me into the waltz. It took me a few seconds to recognize Zee. It actually made sense. They'd come into the dance together so one would follow the other in the pattern. I didn't try pulling Zee. She was much smaller than Genevieve, and I was worried I'd somehow break her if I tried. Not that my efforts would do anything, anyway. As Genevieve had said, I couldn't break the magic with brute force.

"I'm sorry," I whispered, barely audible over the music. Zee must have heard me nevertheless because she said something herself. "Stop the music." Her words ran quickly together, and I was already dancing with another partner before they registered in my mind.

Letting go of my current partner's hand, who appeared to be a dozing faerie, I dodged the dancers, skipping and weaving around until I was back next to Orin.

"Enjoy yourself?" he asked darkly.

"It's the music. If we stop the music, the dancing will stop." Glancing around, I couldn't see the source of the music, but after closing my eyes and listening, I realized it was coming from above. Opening my eyes, I peered above me and spotted a couple of leprechauns sitting on worn wooden stools on a raised platform above the dancers. One played the fiddle, the other a flute.

The platform hung by four ropes from a large branch. Most would find getting up there difficult, but I knew I could do this. Now was my time to shine. Taking a good run up, I darted to the tree, and using momentum, propelled myself upwards, using the knots in the wood as hand and footholds. I was up the tree in seconds and from there, it was pretty easy to walk along the thick branch. When I was directly above them, I dropped myself down, landing right on top of the pair of them. One rolled off as the platform swung wildly, but the other, the one with the flute, managed to carry on playing despite falling face down. All he'd done was cock his head to the side and keep the tune going.

I grabbed the flute from his hands and flung it over the platform into the fire. There was a deathly silence, and then all hell broke loose. The people below me began to scatter in all directions, finally free of the spell that had bound them. I lowered myself off the edge of the platform and dropped. In the chaos, I spotted Zee. Running to her, I grabbed her arm and pulled her through the confusion to Orin who actually managed to look impressed.

I glanced back at the mess of people scurrying this way and that to find Genevieve. She wasn't difficult to spot. She might not have Zee's fiery red hair, but she was a good deal taller than many of the faerie folk. I spotted her looking nervous at the other side of the bonfire. Tapping Orin's shoulder, I pointed her out through the flames of the bonfire, which were the only thing in the party still dancing.

I was just about to guide Zee and Orin through the madness when a huge voice boomed out, echoing through the night. The faeries still left began to scream, running even faster than they were before, despite bloody and blistered feet. I turned my eyes to the source of the noise and saw the strangest and most terrifying being I'd ever laid eyes on.

He must have been seven feet tall with a crown made from deer antlers and a thick coat of fur. His chin sported a long black goatee, and matching hair like Spanish moss trailed down his back. None of that frightened me though. It was his eyes. He had no pupils or irises at all, only whites, and though it was hard to tell, I had the feeling he was looking right at me.

"Let's get out of here," Orin cried, grabbing Zee's and my hands in his and guiding us through the throng toward the large hedge that ran around the Erl-King's garden.

I steered us slightly to the left so we could pick up a startled Genevieve along the way.

I didn't need to look behind me to know the Erl-King was following us. I could hear the boom of his feet as they hit the dirt beneath him.

"Quicker!" I hissed, practically dragging Zee who was having trouble keeping up with us.

The Erl-King's stride was as long as a giant's. He'd catch us. "Who spoiled my party?" His voice boomed out into the night, sending a shudder down my spine.

At the hedge, I turned and faced him. He was almost upon us. Just another few steps and we would be in his clutches. Adrenaline pumped through my veins, triggering a fight or flight reaction. My back was to the hedge, so flight was no longer an option. I had only one option left. He was bigger than me and much bulkier, but I'd learned in my stunt training that his size could be used to my advantage. I brought myself up to my full height and screamed, readying myself to launch at him. I coiled my muscles to jump when I felt myself being pulled backwards through a hole in the hedge. I fell to the ground with a thunk, landing, thankfully, on a patch of soft dirt.

The hole we'd just come through sealed back up, trapping the Erl-King in his own garden. His bellow of anger at the loss of his prey rattled my eardrums.

The chill of the night enveloped me as the warmth of the bonfire disappeared.

"Are you freaking insane?" Orin spat at me. "You weren't seriously going to fight the Erl-King?"

"Someone had to," I countered, getting to my feet and dusting the dirt off of me.

For a second I thought I might have seen admiration in his eyes.

"Let's go," Zee said, taking off across the meadow. I had no idea where she was heading, but as it was away from the Erl-king's castle, it was good enough for me.

The meadow was actually a field filled with a strange grass-like crop so tall the plants hid us easily. We ran through the plants for an hour before Orin shouted at all of us to stop. He might have been good with magic, and there was no doubt that it had been he that saved us back there, but he did not have the stamina of the rest of us. The poor guy looked exhausted.

"He won't find us now," Orin wheezed, plunking down in the grass. He pulled the apple out of his backpack and stared at it. The second clue! In all the excitement, I'd completely forgotten we'd gotten it. Genevieve delved into her backpack and brought out another apple which she held up next to Orin's.

Besides their golden color, they looked utterly unremarkable.

"I hope we didn't go through all that just to have stolen the Erl-King's fruit basket," I said, only half-jokingly.

"These have known magic," Orin replied sniffing the fruit. He rubbed his hands over it, and the air crackled, but nothing happened. The apple remained very apple-like.

"I think we have to eat it," Orin ventured after exhausting his other avenues of bringing the magic out of it.

Both Genevieve and Zee shook their heads violently. I could quite understand why. The last time they'd eaten something from the Erl-King's house, they'd been trapped in an enchanted dance. I wasn't eager to try it out either, despite the pain in my rumbling empty stomach.

Orin bit into the flesh of the apple. The three of us watched him carefully as he munched his way through to the core. Nothing happened. Absolutely nothing at all.

"I guess it was just an apple after all," I cried, horror filling me. Had we missed the real clue somehow? Or had Orin...eaten it? "But why? There were six on those little platforms. And...gold!"

Zee threw her apple to the ground, baring her teeth with her sharp canines. "Crap. We're going to have to go back to the Erl-King's castle!"

Genevieve looked anything but happy at the prospect, and I shared her assessment.

"Not so fast!" Orin broke the core in two and pulled out the seeds. Pushing them into the dirt by his feet, he stood up and took a step back. "Water?"

"I have a little," Zee said, reluctantly pulling a canteen from her bag and passing it to Orin who sprinkled the contents on top of the seeds. Almost instantly, there was a rumble from the earth below us, and a tree began to sprout from the earth.

We all stumbled back, and less than two minutes later, we were found ourselves standing under the canopy of an enormous apple tree. About halfway up protruded a branch in the shape of an extended arm. It even had a finger that pointed a little to our left. Without a word, I shimmied up the tree to see over the tall crops. About two miles ahead in the direction the tree pointed, past a mass of trees, was a strange looking hill. As it was the only thing I could see on the horizon, I figured that was our destination.

Zee called up to me. "What do you see?"

"I see a hill, but it's not normal. It's pink!" It looked as if it were covered in a blanket of flowers.

"Oh, a faerie hill!" Zee clapped her hands together and bounced up and down on the balls of her feet.

I was just about to jump down to join them when a thought struck me. I was surrounded by the largest juiciest apples I'd ever seen.

"You can pick them!" Orin called up, answering my unasked question. "I'm pretty sure they're edible."

Instead of picking them one by one, I shook the branches near me, sending fruit raining down.

Below me, the three of them dodged the falling apples before bending over and filling their backpacks with the fruit.

I pulled the last one I could reach from the tree and took a bite. It was the most delicious thing I'd ever tasted.

"Thank you for your help," Genevieve said gruffly as I swung down and landed right next to her. Her cheeks were rosy. I could tell she was embarrassed that they had needed help. "Here. I think you should have this."

It was the original magic apple they'd taken from the castle.

"It might come in handy if you are hungry later in the race," she continued.

To the side of her, Zee nodded.

I took it and put it in my own backpack. I wasn't going to

look a gift horse in the mouth, and thanks to us, they already knew where they needed to go next.

"But this is a race, after all. I think it's time for us to go our own separate ways."

I nodded reluctantly. It would be nice to have someone around other than broody Orin, but I knew it was for the best.

Genevieve held out her hand, and I shook it. Zee followed suit, shaking first my hand, then Orin's.

With a wave and a smile, they ran off into the grass towards the faerie hill.

"What now?" I asked.

Orin shrugged his shoulders. "I guess we carry on with the race." He picked up a final couple of apples, and the two of us ventured onwards.

16

——

Orin and I walked through the dark wood, munching our third and fourth apples, respectively. Already my stomach twisted in protest of the strange meal, but I didn't care. I was tired of the feeling of emptiness in my belly. At this point, even the leaves on the trees were looking good. Was lettuce really so different?

A thought gnawed at me, refusing to go away. I shoved it to the back of my mind, but it kept rearing its head. I looked sidelong at Orin, trying to think of any other way than asking *him* for help. But I couldn't see it. He was the only resource I had in here, the only thing close to an ally. I had to, at least, ask. "I think I need to learn magic," I finally blurted.

"No shit, Sherlock," he replied, tossing an apple core over his shoulder and wiping his sticky hands on his pants.

I rolled my eyes at him. Of course, he knew that literary reference. I forged ahead. "What you did back there with the hedge—I need to be able to do things like that. If something happened to you..."

"Plan on ditching me?" he asked.

"No," I said. "I'm just saying...if you were sick...or injured. If I needed to help us escape—"

"It still amazes me that you went through an entire month of training and you have the magical ability of a rock. Less than some rocks actually. How is that possible?"

I scowled.

"You did magic at the final trial," Orin said. "Why don't you just build on that?"

My eyes flicked to Ben and his blinking light. I didn't want to admit that Tristam had done the magic that had gotten me through. I didn't think the FFR execs would pull me at this point in the race, but I couldn't risk it. Not when I'd already come so far.

"I can't recreate it," I admitted, searching for an excuse. "I'm not sure why. Maybe under pressure, I summoned something that I can't now."

"You don't consider *this* under pressure?" He gestured to the ominous forest around us, where at any moment, some toothy faerie monster could leap out and attack.

"You know what I mean. Fine. Forget I said anything." Why had I thought this was a good idea again?

"Wait a minute," he said his eyebrows quirking. He looked almost cute when he did that. I banished the thought with horror. Orin—cute? Absolutely not. Orin had been nothing but an ass to me since we met. "Are you asking me for help?" he continued. "Is the great Jacqueline Cunningham admitting there is something she can't do better than everyone else?"

I punched him in the arm with all my might. Wish it could be his smug face, I thought savagely. "Only when it comes to magic. In all other arenas, I'm vastly superior to you."

"Including humility."

I wanted to scream. "Will you help me or not?"

"I will. But I'm going to make you suffer for it a bit longer."

I let out an incredulous laugh. "I don't think you're supposed to admit your devious plan."

"Just another thing I'm not as good at as you," he said.

"Indeed," I countered with a toothy grin.

He looked around. We were in a sparse stretch of forest that looked slightly less forbidding than the rest of the thick foliage we'd been traipsing through. We had to be almost all the way to the faerie hill. "Maybe we should stop for the night," he suggested. "We don't know what we're going to face in there. It wouldn't hurt to tackle it on a full night's sleep."

That sounded like sense to me. "I agree. It's been too easy to get from the Erl-King's castle to the hill. There will be some sort of nasty surprise before we get the next clue."

Orin laid out his sleeping bag while I gathered some kindling and dry brush for the fire and tried not to be too annoyed that I didn't have a sleeping bag of my own. It's not like we had anything to cook for dinner, but it would be nice to be warm for a change.

"All right, start the fire," Orin said.

I looked at him. "You have the magic."

"I thought you wanted to learn."

I snorted. "We're going to be here forever if that's how you're trying to teach me. I tried with Evaline for about the entire month of training and failed at every point." Though I had been successful that time with Tristam on the roof.

"Just show me," he said.

"Fine." I sat down cross-legged and gazed at the fire. I pulled memories of warmth to me—a toasty fire in the lodge at Big Sky ski resort, a hot shower after a long day of training, that week last year when we all thought the entire city of L.A. was going to melt. God, what I wouldn't give to be in any of those situations over this one...I banished that thought as I felt the warmth building inside me, focusing on the heat. But when I tried to release it as Tristam had shown me, nothing happened.

I opened my eyes with a huff.

Orin was studying me like a science project.

"What?" I asked self-consciously.

"What do you do to when you try to light it?"

I furrowed my brow, looking for words. "I try...to light it. I imagine myself lighting it. I shove my hot thoughts towards it—"

"Your hot thoughts?" He chortled.

I hissed. "You know what I mean. I try to see it in my mind. Will it to happen."

"Hmm." He stroked his chin like a detective from a cheesy movie. "That might be your problem. You can't... force magic. You're not its master. It's a partnership of equals. You have to surrender to it. Trust it."

"Trust it? Hell no. This stuff ruined my sister's life."

Orin's eyes widened, and I cursed my slip. I shouldn't have mentioned Cass. "Your sister had a bad experience with magic?"

"I don't want to talk about it."

"You don't have to tell me what happened. But...how did it make you feel?"

"You're not my shrink, Orin. How the hell do you think it made me feel? I never wanted anything to do with the stuff ever again."

He nodded. "I think you might have blocked yourself."

"What do you mean?" My ears perked. This was new.

"Your fear of magic is keeping you from fully surrendering to it. Imagine you have...walls around you that you've built for what you think is your protection. You need to take its hand, but you can't do that from inside your fortress."

"I'm not afraid of it," I said. "I just don't want anything to do with it."

"Me thinks thou doth protest too much..." he said, giving me a tight-lipped smile.

"Shut it, Shakespeare," I snapped. I chewed on what he said, turning it over in my mind. I wasn't afraid of magic, was I? I was just being cautious to stay away from something that had hurt Cass. It was self-preservation, not fear. Right? The sentiment rang false within me. Maybe I was afraid. Just a little. "If you were right...which I'm not saying you are," I hurried on, "What do you suggest I do?" I hated that I needed his help. I hated that I needed magic.

"You need to get over your fear."

"Oh, okay, I'll just...do that." My fists balled at my side.

Orin sat down on his sleeping bag across the dark pile of kindling. "Jacq, when it comes to things like fighting a crocodile to save a girl you've just met or battling ancient forest kings, you're the most fearless human I've ever met. And humans have no reason to be fearless. You're incredibly easy to kill."

"You flatter," I said dryly.

Orin went on. "It's the truth. But for whatever reason, nothing scares you."

"Except this," I admitted quietly.

"When I was a kid," Orin said, "my father told me to pretend magic was my...pet." He closed his eyes as if embarrassed to admit this.

"Your pet?" I laughed.

"Yes. All types of pets, really. You know about the five elements, right?"

"I'm not a complete magical dunce, thank you."

"Just checking. Well, he told me to think of each of the elements as a pet. Fire was a little dragon, obviously."

"Like Mushu from *Mulan*?" I asked. That was one of Cass's and my favorite movies as a kid. A pang went through me at the thought.

"I have no idea what you just said. But...sure," Orin said. "Water was a fish. Air was a hawk, and Earth was a rabbit. It made magic feel...familiar. Friendly even. The elements don't want to work with someone who doesn't want to work with them."

"You make it sound like magic is easily offended."

"It has a personality. I mean, sure, the magician shapes the magic. But in its essence, it's playful. Lively."

"That doesn't sound so bad," I admitted. "And what about quora? That's the faerie life force, right?"

"Yes. My father told me to imagine quora as me. A... spirit version of myself. To hang out with my element pets. Together, we could...do things." He rubbed his brow, not meeting my eyes.

"That sounds...really sweet, actually," I said. "Where's your dad now?"

Orin's mask slammed back into place. "I don't want to talk about it." It seemed that I wasn't the only one with secrets.

I recoiled at his fierceness, searching for a safe subject. "So you think I should think of magic as a pet?"

"I don't know. I haven't thought about that in years. But it helped me not be afraid of it. Maybe it will help you." With that, I could tell that our conversation was over. Orin lay down, crawled into his sleeping bag. and rolled over, his broad shoulders a wall between us.

Just before he began to snore, I saw the flick of his hand over his shoulder.

The fire before me burst into a cheerful blaze, banishing the chill of the night. Next to me on the dirt lay a new sleeping bag, in all its downy glory. With a smile, I crawled into it, zipping it up all the way. As I drifted off to sleep, images of magic bunnies danced around me.

17

Orin shook me awake the next morning. I was stiff, and my stomach was unhappy from the all-apple dinner we'd enjoyed last night. But over-all, it wasn't the worst night I'd had over the Hedge. At least I'd been warm.

"I found a good vantage point to scope out the faerie hill. I think we should get moving."

"Okay," I said, reveling in the last moment before I unzipped my sleeping bag and let all the cold air in. Before, I might have made a snide remark, but last night we'd seemed to form an uneasy truce, and I was loathe to break it. It was a relief to feel, for a change, like I had a partner. That I wasn't in this strange place entirely alone.

He threw something at me, and it took a second to register what it was. A packet of Oreo cookies? A bunch of berries I might have understood, but Oreos? I opened my mouth to question him, but he held his forefinger to his lips and pointed at the bag of the sleeping Ben. It was open. Orin had stolen the cookies. Normally I'd have been as angry as all hell, but I was so hungry that I found I didn't care. Pulling open the pack, I shoveled three in my mouth at once, savoring the chocolaty taste and passed the pack to Orin.

"Very ladylike," he whispered, taking one cookie and chewing on it.

We ate the full pack before quietly zipping Ben's bag back up and waking him from his sleep. He'd notice they were gone later, but as a cameraman, he'd be able to get more.

We packed up our meager camp and trudged up a little hill to an outcropping at the edge of the forest. The thick trees opened up to a soft rolling hill that sloped down before us, leading to a grassy meadow. The faerie hill hunched in the middle of it, covered in a riot of flowers.

"It's beautiful," I admitted.

"Beautiful, and deadly. These are places of great power. Usually, that attracts powerful faeries."

Great.

"Best to stay out of sight." Orin knelt down and took my hand, pulling me down beside him. I huffed but relented, lying out on my stomach beside him in the dewy grass like a sniper, trying to ignore the familiarity of his motion and how it made my already-queasy stomach flip.

"Do we see anything that could be a clue?" I squinted, trying to spot anything out of the ordinary. Or...*more* out of the ordinary. Because everything seemed weird in this back-ward place.

"It won't be outside. It will be underneath."

"Underneath?" I asked. "You can go inside that thing?"

"The hills are gateways. Many faeries live below ground. There are vast networks of tunnels. Worlds you don't see."

That was a disconcerting thought—there could be

hostile faeries walking beneath us right now. "Do you see...a door then?"

"I don't. It could be on the other side. I suggest we make a lap. But keep our distance."

A sound of cracking branches reached our ears, and Orin seized me, slapping a hand over my mouth, and pulling me even further down into the tall grass.

I froze, partially in surprise at his closeness. This close he smelled of the forest—herby smells like sage and mint and fresh-turned soil.

Out of the tree line tromped Yael and Duncan. Yael had tied his long white-blond hair in a braid over one shoulder, and with his pale skin, he shone nearly white in the morning sun. He strode with that proud swagger that I was beginning to recognize as a faerie trademark. He walked as if he owned the whole world, and it was here to serve him.

Duncan at his side moved more cautiously, his head swiveling as if entering enemy territory. I suppose it was all enemy territory. But still, he kept his dark eyes sharp above the shadow of a beard that was coming in.

Orin removed his hand from my mouth, shifting imperceptibly away from me.

As the team moved closer to the faerie hill, Yael gestured in a pattern I didn't recognize. The blanket of flowers parted, revealing a wooden door on the side of the hill facing us.

It reminded me of a scene from Lord of the Rings. But I knew that there was no hobbit inside.

"Let's go," I said. "We can go in after them."

Orin shook his head. "Let's see what happens. I don't trust Yael not to betray us."

Funny, that's how I felt about all the faeries. But, there must be something extra about Yael that Orin didn't like. "We don't know how he made the door appear," I protested.

"What if it disappears? We could miss our chance." I tried again to stand, but Orin grabbed my arm, pulling me back down. "Wait," he hissed.

"What?" I looked back, and my eyes widened. He was right. Amongst the blanket of reds and pinks and magentas...something was moving.

"They wouldn't," Orin said, his eyes growing wide with horror.

"What?"

Yael and Duncan were just feet from the door when an explosion of movement burst forth from the blossoms. Dozens—hundreds of tiny creatures with pointed red hats swarmed at them.

"What the hell are those?" I asked. They were like... garden gnomes. If garden gnomes had razor sharp teeth and bulging white eyes.

"Red Caps," Orin breathed.

The creatures swarmed around Yael and Duncan in a racing circle. The competitors raised their hands, and magic crackled the air around them. A protective bubble of magic materialized around the faerie and the man.

"What are Red Caps?" I whispered, mesmerized by the sight of the little creatures moving in tandem. They were like a swarm...ants...or bees?

"They're like..." Orin searched for the right word. "Piranhas. They're flesh eating. Once they have your scent, you're done for. I can't believe they put the clue directly under a nest."

"Those things...eat people?" I swallowed. Flesh-eating garden gnomes. Leave it to Faerwild.

Orin looked directly into the camera that Ben held a few feet away, talking to the show producers. "You guys are bastards."

The circle around Yael and Duncan was growing smaller as the swarm tightened, surging against the magic—testing the defenses. Where a Red Cap brushed against it, the bubble would flash with light like a bug zapper.

Yael held up his hands, maintaining the shield, while Duncan flung magic through it—lightning bolts that sent the Red Caps sailing into the air. But there were so many of them. "There's no way he can get them all," I whispered, paralyzed by the sight before me.

Duncan seemed to realize the same thing and sent out a spell like a shock wave, knocking the Red Caps off their feet. But more came. With every creature that Duncan killed, it seemed two more took its place.

"We need to help them," I said, pushing to my feet, realizing with horror how this scene would end. "They're going to die."

"We can't help everyone," Orin protested. "They got themselves into this mess by bumbling forward like a couple of idiots."

"How can you be so heartless?" I rounded on him.

He faced me, staring me down. "I'm not heartless. I'm just not willing to sacrifice what I care about for strangers. They're our competition."

"What do you care about?" I scoffed. "Seems to me to be one thing. Orin Treebaum. Stay here if you want. But I'm going to help."

One of the Red Caps had made it through Yael's magic shield now, and darted at Duncan, latching onto his shin. He bellowed in pain as I lunged down the hill.

Orin's strong arms caught me around my waist and hauled me back into the grass. "No!" he shouted as I struggled against him, trying to scramble out from under him. "I let you save Genevieve. I'm not letting you save them. I can't lose you," he said, his dark eyes burning like stars as he looked at me.

His words stunned me, shaking me back to myself. I froze.

"You can't...lose me?" Was it possible that somehow, Orin had actually come to care for my safety?

"If you die...I lose the race," he stammered, leaning back on his heels, putting distance between us.

Reality slammed back into me. "Right," I said, realizing my assessment of him was all too true.

Another Red Cap had made it through Yael's protective enchantment, and Yael pulled out his sword and sliced it in two. But it seemed the creatures who had made it through had weakened the field, and now the little faerie bastards began pouring through.

Yael and Duncan shouted in dismay, swinging swords and shooting magic.

"I can't watch," I said, my stomach churning.

"If they're in danger, they can use their emergency beacon," Orin said. "They'll forfeit the race, but they'll live. It's their choice to still be there. Don't put this on yourself."

I turned away, my hands hovering over my eyes. Of all the things that I thought might happen in my life, watching someone be eaten alive by tiny, bloodthirsty monsters was definitely not one of them. "And you wonder why I'm afraid of magic?" I said, fighting back tears.

I risked a peek through my fingers just as Yael and Duncan's protective bubble failed. The Red Caps swarmed them.

But suddenly, a bright purple light shot into the sky. Instantly, a faerie in a gray uniform with the FFR logo appeared in the sky, hovering like an avenging angel. He shot a spell on the scene below that froze every single Red Cap.

"They gave up," I let out an incredulous laugh, relief surging through me like a powerful tide. "They're going to be okay."

"This is our chance," Orin said, his voice surging with excitement. His words were muddled in my mind. I didn't understand.

"The door is right there. The Red Caps are frozen. Come on!" Before I could think, he took my hand and pulled me to my feet, dragging me forward into a full sprint towards the faerie hill.

18

Getting inside the hill was surprisingly easy. I guess the obstacle was the Red Caps which, thanks to Yael and Duncan, we didn't have to deal with.

I was feeling decidedly happier as Orin closed the door behind us. Two contestants were out of the race, which gave us two less people to worry about.

The room we'd walked into was really nothing more than an opening carved out of the hillside. The walls were mud and dirt, and the roots of plants and flowers hung from the ceiling above us. It smelled musty, of wet earth; although, the ground beneath my boots was dry. The only object of interest in the whole room was a mirror. With an antique gold frame, the floor length mirror was completely incongruent with its surroundings. It would have been better suited to a stately hotel than a hole in the ground, which is, essentially, what we were in.

"The next clue has something to do with the mirror," exclaimed Orin, peering at his own reflection.

"What was it you said to me earlier? No shit, Sherlock?"

Orin narrowed his eyes at my reflection behind him.

"It seems we aren't the only ones to get here either." I nodded to the floor beside the mirror. There were two contestants' backpacks tucked behind the mirror, barely noticeable in the dim light. Two bags, but no people.

"Where are they?" asked Orin, peering around the dark room. There was very little light, but the room was so small that it was obvious there was no one else here but Orin and me.

I looked over at Orin and gazed over his shoulder. A pair of intense eyes glared back at me, and I was shocked to find that they were my own. Did I really look that way nowadays? Thin and angry, a little wild? Pulling my features into a more suitable expression, I sidestepped Orin and touched the cold glass of the mirror. My reflection did the same, but there was something not quite right about it. It took me a few seconds before I realized what it was. Behind my reflection, almost invisible, was a lever in the dirt wall. Checking over my shoulder, I scanned the wall. There was no lever— yet it was definitely there in the reflection.

I backed up, keeping my eyes on mirror me and felt along the dirt wall. There was nothing there, but my reflection definitely had hold of something. I mimed pulling down and watched as my reflection pulled the lever. Immediately, the surface of the mirror began to shimmer. My reflection was still there, now complete with a self-satisfied smirk, but she was hazy with a slight ripple effect over her.

Orin goggled at me, and I couldn't help myself. I shot him a wink and walked right up to the mirror.

"What are you doing?" Orin asked as I pressed my finger up to the watery surface.

I turned to face him. "Haven't you ever read *Alice through the Looking Glass*?" As I said it, a very strong memory of Cass and I reading it together by flashlight under the covers when we were little hit me right in the pit of my stomach. Why was it that my memories of her were stronger than ever? Ever since we'd come into Faerwild, my dreams of her had gotten more intense. I could almost feel her, reach out to her, and touch her, but she was not there. She was never there. I felt like she was walking with me through this strange land. It was almost as though the FFR knew about her, but there was no way they could...was there?

"Alice who?"

"You've heard of some old German poet, and you've heard of Sherlock, but not Alice?" I narrowed my eyes at him. How was it possible to know about a fictional London detective and not a classic fairytale?

"Actually, I don't know what a Sherlock is, I just heard the saying, but that hasn't answered my question. What are you doing?"

I shook my head in disbelief. He knew about as much about the human world as I did about Faerwild. I wondered how he'd fare if he had to cross one of Burbank's busy streets to buy a round of coffees for a bunch of studio execs. Now that really was a challenge!

"I'm going in." I pressed my hand forward, and as I expected, it passed through the shimmering surface as easily as dipping my hand into a pond.

And without waiting for his objection, I walked through the magical surface of the mirror. Or...I tried. When my backpack hit the mirror, it seemed to resist moving through. I backed up, unshouldering my pack and tossing it behind the mirror with the two others. Apparently, where we were going, we couldn't take supplies.

I pushed through again, and a cold shiver passed through me before I found myself in an identical room to the one I'd just left...although, now I was standing next to the mirror Orin. He copied the exact movements of the real Orin at the other side of the glass. It was weird. It was like there were two of him, but only one of me. I was quite glad when the real Orin plucked up the courage to follow me through.

I looked back to see Ben pushing through with his red-blinking camera light, coming out the other side with no problem. Yet another rule of the race that didn't apply to him, I guess.

"What is this place?" Orin asked. "There are legends of faerie paths that could be accessed through mirrors, but I always thought that was an old wives' tale." I could see the fear in his eyes.

"Maybe you should start thinking of those fluffy bunnies again," I replied, stepping towards the door. Either it would be an exact, but opposite replica of outside, or, like Alice's looking glass world, it would be completely different. When I opened the door, I saw that it was firmly in the second category, but this was no wonderland.

My heart seized in my chest. It was my bedroom. Not the one I had in the apartment I shared with Christine, but the small attic bedroom Cass and I shared as kids. My heart jumped into my throat as I took in the detail around me. It was exactly the same down to the faint smell of perfume that had lingered for months after Cass stole a bottle of our mother's favorite perfume and accidentally spilled it all over the carpet. I ran to the bed and threw back the covers hoping I'd find Cass there, but there was only Peaches, the raggedy doll she used to insist was hers, but really, it had been given to me by my mother when I'd fallen out of a tree and broken my ankle. We'd fought for so long over that stupid doll...I think it had ended up in the garbage about the time we got interested in boys, and our childhood toys meant nothing to us anymore. Now, I wished more than anything that I still had Peaches. I picked up this mirror copy and held it close to me.

"This was my room. I shared it with Cass...my sister."

I walked to the bedside table and noticed a book with a strange symbol on the front—one of Cass's. I recognized it immediately, but it was out of place in this room. The timeline was wrong. Peaches had stayed with us throughout our childhood, but I'd only seen Cass with this book when we were much older—when she started working with her coven. I'd known it had something to do with magic, but I'd never asked her about it. Now I wished I had. For it was the one thing the ICCF had taken from our house when they questioned us about her disappearance.

My heart leapt into my throat as I picked it up. The ICCF had refused to tell us why they were confiscating the book or why it was important to their investigation. We'd never gotten any answers. I opened the book, wondering if it would finally provide some clue as to why she left or where she went, but all the pages were blank. The only thing I found inside was an origami flower. Smiling, I remembered it well. It was how the two of us passed secret notes to each other, hidden in plain sight. I unfolded the flower carefully and on the back in childish writing were the words *LOVE U JACQ.*

It was only when Orin asked why I was crying that I realized I had tears running down my face.

I felt closer to her here than I had since the day she left. It was almost as though she was within reach.

With that thought in mind, I jumped up and ran to the other door in the room. Behind it, stood the stairs that led down to the home we lived in until I'd moved to L.A., wanting more than anything to leave Montana, and its memories of Cass, behind. The stairs were exactly the same as I remembered, down to the creak on the third one from the bottom, but when I stepped into the room that should have been the living room with its rustic fireplace and my dad sitting on his Lazy-z-Boy chair filling in the crossword and my mother reading some soap opera digest, instead I found a long dining room.

I skidded to a halt, almost dropping Peaches on the floor as I took in the scene in front of me. The room was almost macabre with its long black table and gothic architecture. It reminded me of a room in a haunted house.

"No...no, no, no."

I turned to find Orin staring past me, his eyes wide. The fear I'd seen in them before was nothing to what I was seeing now. He looked positively terrified.

"I can't be here, this place was destroyed..." His words were a whisper, almost too quiet to make out. "I burned it."

I recoiled, looking at him. So this was a place from his past? That's what the mirror did. It took you to places of high emotion in your past. In my case, it reminded me of a better time, a time before Cass disappeared. If any memory was sure to get me, it'd be one with Cass.

Judging by Orin's face, his memory was much more sinister. He'd destroyed this room? I wondered why, but couldn't find the words to ask him. Not in front of the cameras. Not here.

Instead, I tried to bring him back to the situation at hand. "This isn't real. We just need to find the clue. For a minute back there, I thought it had taken us back in time, but I think the mirror shows what's in our heads. For me, it took me back to my happiest place."

"Lucky you," snapped Orin, "because it's brought me to

my worst nightmare. I need to get out of here. He'll be back in a minute."

"Who?"

I followed Orin's gaze to the door at the other side of the room. Something behind that door terrified him. Whatever it was, it was from Orin's past, not mine, and so I wasn't scared of it. I left Orin where he was and marched past the long table to the door. When I opened it, I wished I hadn't.

Cass was standing there. My breath hitched in my chest at the sight of her. But not in surprise and delight—in horror! She looked nothing like I remembered her. Gone was the youthful beauty with hope on her face and light in her eyes. Now she was pale and painfully thin with welts and scars all the way up her arms and legs. Manacles on her wrists and ankles tethered her to the wall. All she wore was a dirty rag tied around herself. When she looked up, her eyes locked on mine. She opened her mouth and began to scream. My blood surged through my body in double quick time. I needed to get to her! As I stepped into the room, a tall faerie male with heavy features and thick eyebrows materialized, swinging a sword at me.

The faerie sliced at me with his blade, but I was too quick for him. Despite his height, he was almost as thin as Cass, and his movements were slow.

I reached Cass, but there was nothing I could do for her with the crazy man swinging his sword around. I ducked again, weaving under his bony arms as he swung the sword around and around, trying in vain to hit me.

I screamed out, adding to Cass's voice. Out of the corner of my eye, I saw a flash of black.

Orin pushed me to one side as the man swiped at me with his sword.

"You didn't beat me the first time, you'll not do it now,"

screamed Orin, lunging at the male, sending him to the ground. The sword clattered to the floor with a loud clang. Both Orin and the old man turned their heads from their positions on the floor to look at it.

Orin lunged for the sword, his fingers closing around it. He reared back and plunged it into the faerie's chest.

"Thank you!" I called out, relieved it was over. "We need to free Cass."

Orin swung the sword down towards the manacles chaining her to the wall, but at the last second, he changed trajectory, and the sword went clean through Cass's neck, sending her head flying across the room.

Somewhere, someone screamed, and it took me a few seconds to realize it was me. All around me, the room was getting hotter. Orin grabbed my hand and tried to pull me back into the weird dining room. "You'll die if you stay here," he shouted as I struggled against him.

My mind was churning, and the pain in my heart was unbearable. I couldn't have come all this way to see my sister die in such a horrific manner.

"You killed my sister!" I screamed as the room heated up even more. What was causing it? I wondered in some recess of my shocked mind.

"Think Jacq!" he yelled back. "That wasn't your sister, and it wasn't...." He trailed off. "All I killed was a figment of both our imaginations. I don't know where your sister is, but she's not in here any more than that male is. But I think there's a fire, a real fire. So let's get a move on before we get roasted."

Cass was still alive? I looked back at her body, uncertainly. "I don't see any flames," I protested, moving back towards her. But the air was feeling thick, and the smell of smoke was overpowering.

"I think someone lit it in the real world," Orin said, taking my hand.

He pulled me forward, and we ran through the dining room and up the stairs that would take us back to the mirror, Ben following close behind. What I wouldn't give for whatever protective enchantments he had.

We dashed through the mirror, into an inferno of flame. The little dirt antechamber was alight with magic flames licking in from the floor to the root-covered ceiling.

Our packs, I thought with horror, but there was no stopping. Not if I wanted to live.

Orin pulled me through the licking flames out the front door to freedom, where I took in great lungfuls of air, patting down my hair and clothes to be sure there were no eager sparks left on me.

Black smoke plumed out of the hillside behind us, so we stumbled up the hill until the air was clear and we were able to breathe.

"We've lost everything," I cried, slumping to the ground and closing my eyes. Weariness threatened to overwhelm me. The memory of Cass, broken and chained, left me hollow and raw. What if that's what she really looked like now? What if she was a prisoner somewhere in Elfame and I was here doing a ridiculous TV show?

"Not quite," I heard Orin say. I opened my eyes to see him examining the sword that he still held in his hand. "This is magic, and I'm pretty sure it's the next clue."

19

We crested the hill into the safety of the trees, away from prying eyes.

"We need to stop for a minute," Ben said, lowering his camera off the rig on his shoulder to the ground. "I think the smoke and heat got to the camera. It's not working."

Orin and I both turned to him. "So the camera is off right now?" I asked.

Ben nodded, and a smile crept onto my face. I felt strangely liberated, knowing no one was watching me. That I could say things that wouldn't be relayed for the whole world to hear.

"So you're going to try to fix it?" Orin asked.

Ben nodded, sitting down cross-legged on the ground, pulling a tiny screwdriver out of his pack. "But if I can't, they'll be along real quick with a new one. They don't want anything going unrecorded."

Orin and I looked at each other helplessly, and I shrugged, sinking onto the ground. I pulled my wild hair out of its ponytail and did my best to comb it with my fingers, braiding it over one shoulder.

Orin was rubbing his face with sooty hands. "I can't believe someone set that fire. Those assholes. It's a race, not the Hunger Games."

"What, that one you've heard of?" I scoffed. "But not Alice?" I shook my head. It didn't matter. "Why do you think someone set the fire? Who?"

"It had to be whatever team went in before us. Their packs were gone. They came out of the mirror with their clue, saw our packs, and knew we were close behind. So they burned everything."

"We could have died!" I said incredulously. Anger bloomed to life in me. "When I find out who did this..." The other competitors raced through my mind. I knew Gen and Zee wouldn't do that, even if they hadn't known it was us in the mirror. Tristam and Sophia? No, they were too cocky to stoop to murder. They thought they had it in the bag. Yael and Duncan were out...Dulcina and Phillip? I just couldn't see a sparkly-purple-haired Pegasus shifter as an attempted murderer. Maybe that was biased...but it left goth-girl Molly and too-sexy-for-his-own-good Ario. "I bet it was Ario and Molly," I said blackly.

"Based on what, your extensive experience profiling?" Orin countered.

"It just...seems like them." I said. "It's always the quiet ones."

"I'm a quiet one," Orin pointed out.

"Exactly," I said under my breath.

Orin sat down across from me, pinning me with his black eyes. They were almost so dark that you couldn't see where the pupil left off and the iris began...but no...there was a slight difference in shade. Deep brown. I blinked and looked at my dirty fingernails, wondering why the hell I was analyzing the color of Orin's eyes.

"You want to tell me what the hell was going on in the mirror with your sister? Is there a reason you think she would be tied up in some faerie dungeon somewhere?"

I looked away, chewing on my lip. I turned back to him. "Is there a reason why you're afraid of some dining room and creepy faerie male that you apparently destroyed?"

Orin met my stare with a challenge of his own. "I'll tell you mine if you tell me yours."

A laugh of disbelief escaped me. I turned away, knowing I had lost our little showdown. "Fine." I looked at Ben. "You're sure that thing is off."

Ben had the back panel of the camera off now, and several pieces were strewn on a handkerchief he had laid out on the dirt. "Yeah, pretty sure, Jacq." He hoisted the dark skeleton of the camera.

"Okay." I took a deep breath. I knew no one over the Hedge but Orin, and I had no idea where to find Cass if I was ever able to get away from the race to look. Maybe Orin could help. Surely stranger things had happened. "My sister was into magic. A few years ago, she met a faerie. She kept it secret, but she started acting strangely. Secretive and weird—we used to tell each other everything, and then, she just clammed up. Two years ago, she disappeared. I think he took her over the Hedge." I closed my eyes against the barrage of memories--police questioning, searching her room, years of missing her.

"That's it?" Orin asked. "Met faerie, disappeared, now you're certain she's here?" He let out a sharp laugh. "Prejudiced much?"

"What other explanation is there?" I said. "She hasn't

contacted us in over two years! If she's safe, if she's free, then why haven't we heard from her?"

Orin's pale brow furrowed in an expression that looked almost like sympathy. His words were soft. "I didn't say she was safe, Jacq. But there have been human murderers and creeps as long as time. What makes you so sure it was a faerie and not some ordinary human wacko?"

I looked away, fighting tears. "She went off with him. I saw them leave together—she told me she was going to be gone a few days and not to say anything. Besides, she was magically talented. She could have fought off a human attacker. Whoever took her had magic stronger than hers. Or had something on her. Was blackmailing her or threatening her or something. I just know it." And then there was that mysterious book and the ICCF investigation. Why would the feds have been nosing around if there wasn't a faerie involved? I wasn't quite ready to tell Orin that part.

"So you're here to find her?"

I nodded, lifting my chin.

"And you have what to go on?"

"If I win the race, I won't need anything to go on. I'll wish for the king to bring her to me safely." I decided to keep to myself the fact that I originally planned to run for it —to find her myself in Faerwild. That plan was feeling more and more foolish the longer I spent over the Hedge. There was no way I'd be able to find her in this place without the boon.

He inclined his head at me.

"What about you, Orin? Who was that man? What was that room?"

Orin looked at Ben and opened his mouth.

Ben beat him to it. "Yes, the camera's off! Jesus, you two seem to think you're hiding state secrets here."

Orin growled softly but turned back to me. "My father was a woodworker. A talented one. The Faerie king wanted him in his royal service, but my father refused. He liked to work for everyone and set his own terms. My mother was a forest elemental. Before I was born, she grew sick, and to save her, my father went to the king for a cure. The king said he'd give him the cure if my father bound himself in service for one hundred years."

"One hundred years!" I said. "That seems a little excessive!"

"You're telling me. But, we live a lot longer than humans. My father was desperate, so he agreed. My mother got better as promised and decided to swear to the king as well so they could spend that time together. She didn't realize she was pregnant. They begged the king to release them from their bond so they could raise their son, but the king said no."

"That was you?"

Orin nodded woodenly. "He kicked me out of his castle. The king didn't want a child of his servants underfoot. I've been...an orphan, basically. My mother's elemental sister raised me when I was young, but the elementals are nomads, and I couldn't live with them forever. Since then, I've been moving between distant relatives to the homes of opportunistic faeries who thought to take advantage of free labor."

"That man...he was one of those?"

Orin rubbed his chin. His eyes were distant as if he was reliving the memories. "One of the worst. He was my great-great uncle. I lived with him for five years until...I couldn't take it anymore."

"I'm sorry, Orin," I said. Somehow, his closed-off demeanor made a lot more sense. Orin hadn't had the upbringing I had, with loving parents and soccer practice and hot chocolate after sledding. He'd had to make it on his own, and it had made him hard.

"Was a long time ago," he replied gruffly, indicating that the subject was closed.

"So you want the wish...to free your parents?" I ventured a guess, moving away from the topic of the man.

He nodded, meeting my eyes. "Eighty-one more years. That's how much longer they'll have to serve that bastard. Unless I do something about it."

"Okay," I said softly, resolve growing in me. "So we win."

I reached out hesitantly and laid my hand over his, where it rested on his knee. "We can do this."

He shook his head angrily, but he didn't move his hand from under mine. "We lost all our supplies. We haven't eaten anything but apples for days."

"It doesn't matter," I said. "We're still in it. We have the sword. You've been through worse than this and survived. And me...well, I'm just awesome."

He looked up in disbelief and found me grinning at him. Orin laughed. "Again with that humility."

"I got it!" Ben cried, startling us apart.

We both looked at him and found him once more behind his camera, the red blinking light recording our every movement. I pulled my hands into the sleeves of my jacket, trying to ignore where my right one had just been.

20

With the weird moment between us now broken, my attention turned to the sword Orin had laid in the grass by his side. I knew a little about swords thanks to working on film sets for various period movies and shows, but this one was like nothing I'd ever seen before. Its long blade curved slightly and was inlaid with some kind of foreign script.

"This looks like a prop from Lord of the Rings," I murmured, wishing that I recognized the strange writing.

"Lord who?" Orin asked, raising an eyebrow.

"Don't tell me you've never heard of Lord of the R...oh, never mind. Do you know what this says? Is it like...Elvish or something?"

Orin took the sword back and examined the length of the blade, running his fingers into the grooves made by the long drawn out shapes.

"It's no language I know, although I do know that Elvish isn't a language. Honestly, did you not read about Faerwild before coming in here?"

I'd read everything I could about this place ever since

my sister had disappeared, but there were very few books on the subject as not many humans had passed through the portal before now, and the fae were not very forthcoming about life here.

"What about the hilt?" I asked, ignoring his snappy attitude. While the blade had been interesting, the hilt was something else entirely. Gold in color, the grip carved into the shape of a dragon with its long tail forming the guard.

"Looks to be something to do with dragons," he said, being deliberately obtuse. At that moment, my stomach grumbled, and I wondered if I was just feeling hangry. It wouldn't be the first time.

Leaving Orin alone with the sword, I scavenged around for something we could eat, some berries at the very least. Finding edible plants wasn't my strong point, but I could recognize a raspberry when I saw one. Unfortunately, raspberries didn't seem to be in plentiful supply here.

I was almost at the point of resorting to pulling bark off a tree and seeing if it was edible when I became aware I was being watched. I stopped still, feeling the hairs on the back of my neck rise. There was definitely something in the woods with me, although I didn't feel the faint crackle of magic that any weird faerie creature would produce.

Keeping my feet steady, I slowly rotated my head, surveying the forest around me. I didn't see it at first, so well was its coat camouflaged in the trees. But when I finally caught sight of a pair of charcoal eyes—and what they were attached to—I ran like hell.

It was a panther.

The big cat crashed through the underbrush after me, closing the distance between us with each powerful bound. I was an excellent runner, even on uneven terrain like this, but I knew there was no way I could outrun a damn panther.

A snarl sounded behind me, so close it made my heart stutter.

But I couldn't look back to see how close it was. To do that would take valuable seconds away from me and I frankly didn't have that many seconds available to me.

I was going to die if I didn't come up with a plan soon. Orin would have just zapped it with his magic or something equally inane, but I didn't have magic at my disposal. I only had myself and my wits. I thought of flinging myself up a tree. If I caught a low branch at the right angle, at this speed, I could swing up and over to safety, but as my dismal luck played out, there were no branches low enough. Plus, couldn't panthers climb trees? Panthers could definitely climb trees.

It was then that I realized with a shock that Orin and Ben were in a clearing directly in front of me. Not only had I put myself in danger, I'd put the guys in danger too. Ben might be all right—he had the protective enchantments keeping him safe, but Orin was going to end up as the main course to my hors d'oeuvres.

I only had seconds left to take action. Even if I ran past Orin, there was no way he'd be able to react in time to get off his ass and throw a spell. Besides, I could hear the panther's ragged breaths right on my heels.

As I crashed into the clearing, I yelled a warning. I only had enough time to take in Orin's crazed expression before I grabbed the sword from his hand and twisted in mid-air. It felt like it happened in slow motion, but in reality, it must have taken less than a few seconds.

As I fell back to the ground, I raised my legs and thrust the sword forward. In the same instant, the panther leapt into the air. The sound as the sword pierced the panther's soft underbelly was haunting. Its cry of pain was followed by the horrible squelch of metal rending flesh and sinew and organs. My feet planted in its underside, allowing me to kick it off to the side as it came crashing down.

It was dead seconds after it hit the ground.

"Bloody hell!" Orin said, standing open-mouthed to one side of me.

To the other, I heard Ben mutter "awesome" from behind his camera.

"Help a girl up?" I asked, trying to look a lot more casual than I felt. "I thought we could eat this for dinner."

I knew how this must look on camera. It might have been a complete accident, but the viewers wouldn't know that. The producers wouldn't know that either. I could almost imagine John peeing his pants at that spectacular piece of footage. I looked like a hero and damn, it felt good after having my ass kicked six ways from Sunday since I set foot in this place.

My only hope was that Ben's camera wasn't too sensitive to sound because from where I was, it felt like a drummer from a rock concert was playing a beat inside my ribcage.

Orin grabbed my hand and pulled me to my feet.

His mouth was still hanging open as I reached for the sword, still buried hilt deep in the panther's chest.

I looked Orin straight in the eye. "We'll need a fire to cook it."

I reveled in the expression on his face—the mixture of awe and incredulity. I shot him a winning grin and turned back to the panther.

I didn't relish the idea of skinning it and cutting up its body for meat, but I was so frickin' hungry, and it was already dead. Leaving it to rot would be a waste. I wasn't a butcher, but I'd been deer hunting a few times with my father and understood the basics of the task. The sword wasn't the best instrument to cut precisely, but it was sharp, and it wasn't too long before we had two slabs of meat cooking on the open fire that Orin had magicked up.

I'd never considered panther a meat I'd try, but it smelled delicious. Orin tended to the meat as I began the task of cleaning the panther's blood off the sword using a couple of leaves. It was either that or using the clothes I was wearing, and they were filthy enough as it was.

As I wiped the leaves down the blade, something peculiar began to happen. As expected, the blood sank into the grooves of the strange language, but it followed other paths too. Grooves I'd not seen originally were now beginning to appear thanks to the panther's blood.

I didn't say anything to Orin as I pushed the blood, concentrating on the line of symbols, and when I'd finished, the words looked completely different. Though, unfortunately, they looked equally as undecipherable as they had before the other parts of the letters had appeared.

I scrutinized the sword, trying to decipher what the strange elongated letters meant. There was something oddly familiar about them. I traced my fingers along the first letter if that's what it was. It was comprised of a long straight line, with a much shorter line at a ninety-degree angle on top. It almost looked like the uppercase letter T except it was so tall and thin. Something registered in the back of my mind. I had seen this script before after all.

As a child, Cass had a book on optical illusions. She was obsessed with them, and I think it's what led her to becoming involved in magic. In the book, was a word. It was written in English but was impossible to read as the letters were extremely thin and tall. The only way to read the word was to hold the book up and tilt it backwards, shortening the perspective of the word and making it readable. No wonder I'd recognized this language. It wasn't Elven or elvish, or whatever it was called, it was written in plain English. As I tilted the sword, hope and excitement fluttered in my chest. If I was right, not only would I have saved his life and brought him dinner, I'd also beat Orin to figuring out the next clue. With a grin, I read at the words. *Dragon's Keep on Emerald Mountain.* That's all it said, but it was enough.

Giddiness flooded me as I laid the sword on the grass beside me and rubbed vigorously until the blood came off and the blade appeared shiny again. I noticed that Ben had the camera trained on Orin and his cooking rather than me so when I told Orin what the next clue was, no one else would know how I managed to figure it out. I stifled a grin as Orin handed me one of the panther steaks.

My stomach flipped at the scent of it, and though it was so hot it almost burned my tongue, I devoured it with gusto, saving just a little for later. I pushed what was left of it into my jacket pocket, which wasn't ideal, but without my pack, it was the only way I had of carrying it.

"We should probably set up camp here while we figure out the clue," Orin said after finishing the last of his steak.

I stood up and sheathed the sword through my belt. I'd never been more aware that I was being broadcast to millions of people. I didn't care much about popularity—that's not why I was in this race, but damn it, I was going to enjoy my moment.

"No need," I said sweetly. "I already figured it out. We're headed to Emerald Mountain."

21

Emerald Mountain was easy to spot, being higher than any of the other hills we'd crossed and getting its name from the brightly colored grass that grew around its base. At least, I assumed that's why it was called Emerald Mountain. For all I knew, it was full of precious gems.

The tall peak loomed over us as we drew closer. Orin trekked silently at my side, and though I knew he was dying to ask me how I'd figured out the clue in the sword, he held his tongue. Stupid male pride.

With my belly filled with a warm meal and our destination in hand, I felt something akin to content. My mind wandered from thoughts of Cass to the other competitors, to Orin's parents—enslaved to the Faerie king. I thought the human realm was a rough place, but at least there, cruelties were usually sharp and short-lived. The fae knew how to make someone suffer for generations.

We passed through the northern edge of the forest into a wide grassland interspersed with rocky outcroppings that stretched to the foot of the mountain.

I paused for a moment to take in the vista. "Wow," I breathed. It was like a painting, undulating green against the blue sky. Well, blue and grey sky. From the east, the sky was turning dark, with threatening black thunderclouds rolling across it. That didn't look fun.

I turned back to the mountain, and the glint of metal caught my eye. I squinted. Far ahead of us, towards the base of the mountain, two tiny figures moved. Other competitors.

"Can you see who that is?" I asked. Perhaps faerie eyesight was better than human.

Orin held his hand up to shield his eyes. "Genevieve and Zee. I can see Zee's red hair."

I nodded, satisfied. I supposed of all the other competitors, I was least bothered by the thought of those two being ahead of us. But not too far ahead.

"Let's go," I said. "See how far we can get before that weather moves in."

Orin and I jogged into the grass; the fresh air and exertion exhilarating me, buoying my spirits. It reminded me of home, well, a freakish, trying-to-kill-you-at-every-turn version of home. The wide-open skies, the scenery painted in sharp colors of green and yellow and brown. Even when the sky darkened, and a cold wind whipped my ponytail, and fat drops began to fall on us, the smile stayed on my face, the endorphins of the run lifting me higher than I'd been in days.

Orin had kept up reasonably well, faerie metabolism and all that, but he was lagging, and I could hear his ragged breathing behind me. "We should find a place to make camp," he said as a bolt of lightning split the sky, followed by a bellow of thunder.

It was as if the sky opened up in answer. A deluge poured down upon us, cold water streaming down our faces, soaking us instantly. I gasped at the shock of it and wiped the water from my face, desperately searching the landscape before us for a place we could shelter out of the weather. "There!" I shouted over the din of the rain. Another fork of lightning exploded above us, illuminating the cluster of rocks above and to the right of us. "I think we could find an overhang there, it should provide some cover."

"Lead the way!" Orin yelled back.

I took off across the slippery terrain towards a wrinkle in the hillside. Skirting along the edge, hopping from slick rock to rock, trying to keep my boots out of the worst of the rushing water, I paused, looking up.

A huge outcropping of boulders loomed above us, still monoliths silhouetted against the dark of the sky. I turned around to find Orin and Ben panting behind me, Orin dripping wet, but Ben completely dry thanks to his protective enchantments. "I think there's a cave up there!"

"Thank god," Orin said. "Let's go."

I picked the rest of the way up carefully, scrambling over a huge boulder, pulling myself up beneath another one that loomed above, blocking the rain. I'd been right. There was a cave here. The relief flooding through me stuttered as I grew nearer and realized that there was a light flickering in the cave. The light of a fire.

I paused, turning to Orin. His dark hair was slicked to his forehead, water cutting rivulets down the hard angles of his cheekbones. "There's someone in there," I said. "They might not be friendly."

"I would fight the Faerie King himself to get dry," Orin said, shaking his hands off. "Let's go. I'm ready."

I felt the same. I was shivering and cold to the bone. We couldn't last a night like this. We'd get hypothermia. I crept around and pulled myself up onto the final ledge that led into the cave. "Hello?" I took a step forward, my hands in fists as I walked around the bend in the cave towards the fire. My eyes widened. "You!" I said, dripping in a puddle on the cave floor.

"You," Tristam said, his finely wrought features twisting into a smile.

"You." Sophia was significantly less excited to see me.

Orin and Ben hauled themselves up onto the ledge, and we moved into the cave, migrating towards the warmth of their fire. It wasn't a huge space, just tall enough to stand in, but it went back a ways to where Sophia and Tristam had set up their fire. Most importantly, it was blessedly dry.

"Come here," Orin said. I turned, and with a motion of his hand, the water drained from my clothes and hair, leaving everything stiff, but dry.

"Thank you," I said, surprised at the kindness.

"This cave is already occupied," Sophia said, her dark eyes flashing at us.

"Nonsense," Tristam replied. "There's plenty of room. No need for you to drown out there."

"Thank you," I said. "We have some food. We'll share." I moved and sat down by the fire, not waiting to be invited. Orin and Ben followed, Ben turning off his camera. Orin had dried them both out too. Tristam and Sophia's camerawoman was sitting in the recesses of the cave, her red light blinking. No need to have two cameras going at once, I guessed.

"How have things been for you two?" Tristam asked, nodding as I passed him a piece of soggy cooked panther meat, pulled from my pocket. I handed one to Sophia too, which she took with a grimace. I guess she didn't hate me enough to reject food.

"Not easy," I let out a laugh. "The first two checkpoints have been no joke."

"The last will be the hardest," Tristam said.

"Did your daddy tell you that?" Orin asked darkly. "You getting behind the scenes info to make sure you get there first?"

"Orin," I exclaimed, shocked at his rudeness. Tristam could have kicked us back into the thunderstorm. I knew how Orin felt about the Faerie king, but there was no need to be a complete dick.

"On the contrary," Tristam said smoothly, not bothered by the slight. "I know nothing more than the rest of the competitors. It was just simple deduction. The hardest challenge always waits at the end."

"Have you run across any other teams?" I asked.

"Dulcina and Phillip near the Erl-King's home. They're ahead of us, I believe."

That was bad news. "Yael and Duncan, briefly as well."

"Poor bastards," Orin muttered under his breath.

"What do you mean?" Sophia asked, leaning forward. Even in a cave, dirty and smeared from travel, she looked beautiful, her thick locks pulled into a braid over her shoulder. I was glad I didn't have a mirror. I was sure I looked like a complete disaster.

"Yael and Duncan are out," Orin said. "The Red Caps got them, and they used their emergency ring."

Tristam whistled. "So then there were ten."

"Genevieve and Zee are ahead of us too," I said. "We saw them further up the mountain this afternoon."

"Then I guess we all better get moving come morning," Tristam grinned.

He was right. We didn't know where Ario and Molly were, but if they were ahead too, then whatever team in this cave got to the third checkpoint last, would be in last place. That wouldn't do.

"Gonna get some sleep," Orin said, clearly done with this conversation. Our sleeping bags had burned in the fire, so he scooted up against the cave wall, crossed his arms over his chest, and closed his eyes. I wondered why he didn't conjure up another one. He had for me, but maybe then he'd have to do the same for Sophia and Tristam and perhaps he wanted them as uncomfortable as we were. Or, perhaps, the spell wasn't as simple as a wave of his hand. I'd have to remember to ask.

TRISTAM OFFERED me a spare jacket as a pillow, which I took gratefully. We all lay down around the fire, which Tristam kept stoked through some magic spell. So, though the ground was hard and rocky, at least I was warm and dry, which I couldn't say for every night over the Hedge.

But still, I couldn't sleep. My mind raced through images of tomorrow, what it could bring. The dragon on the sword worried me. It would be just like FFR to pit us against a dragon for the final showdown of this trial.

Finally, resigned to lack of sleep, I stood, wanting to stretch my sore body. I walked a few steps from the fire towards the mouth of the cave, watching the rain outside. I'd always loved the rain as a kid—there were few things better than watching rivulets pour down the windowpane while snug inside with a blanket and a mug of hot cocoa. It was one of the things I missed in L.A. Rain.

"Hard to believe we've come this far," a voice murmured behind me. I turned to find Tristam joining me.

"It still feels surreal," I agreed, hyper-aware of his presence. He smelled of mint and magic, an intoxicating combination.

"I knew you'd do well. Tell you a secret?"

I raised an eyebrow but nodded.

"Even though you can't do magic to save your life," he whispered, "I wanted you as my partner."

My blood surged in my veins. I licked my lips. "Part of me hoped for that too," I admitted. "Or anyone but Orin." I chuckled softly.

"Has it been awful?"

I considered. "Less awful...than I expected."

"But still. We would have been a perfect match. Your skills and my magic."

"I guess I shouldn't have finished last in training," I said ruefully.

"That was bogus. You are more powerful than any of these humans. More capable. There is something about you Jacq...you are...more alive than other humans I've known."

"Thank you?" I said, warmth blooming in me at the strange compliment. Though, no matter how alive I seemed to Tristam, I was mortal. Which meant I could still end up just as dead.

He turned to me, and my breath caught in my throat. The firelight flickered off the gold in his hair, setting it alight, glowing. It wasn't fair that he was so handsome; it made it impossible for me to focus around him. To think coherent thoughts.

"I want to give you something," he whispered. "Don't tell Sophia, she'd kill me."

He pulled a silver necklace out of his pocket and held it out to me. It swung softy in the air between us. The pendant was an intricate Celtic knot of intersecting and twisting lines. "It's beautiful, thank you," I said, not sure what to say.

"It's not just pretty. It's a talisman. Things are going to get harder before this is done. More dangerous. This will keep you safe. If things get really bad, take it in your hand and say the word 'diogelwch.'"

"Bless you," I joked. It sounded like a sneeze.

"I'm serious," he grinned. "It will protect you. Save you. Now say the word."

"Diogelwch," I said.

"Good." He dropped it into my hand and curled my fingers around it. Then he leaned forward, pressing his lips against my cheek, hot as a brand. I pulled in a breath as he whispered, his words tickling my ear. "I don't want anything to happen to you."

22

I woke up feeling much warmer than I expected to. At first, I thought Tristam's fire might still somehow be lit, but as my fingers curled around something soft, I realized that someone had covered me with a blanket. Tristam?

I opened my eyes to find myself looking at the back of someone's head. Dark waves of hair tickled my nose and left me in no doubt that it was Sophia whose body was practically wedged against me in the small cave. I thought back to the night before.

After coming in from the mouth of the cave, I'd laid myself down next to Orin. To my delight and minor panic, Tristam had lain down on my other side. I'd closed my eyes and pretended to be asleep, my stomach flipping at the thought of being so close to him after what had just happened. He'd kissed me! Okay, so it wasn't on the lips, but he'd given me a talisman, and I hadn't seen one around Sophia's neck.

I'd waited until his breathing had deepened, and only then, did I dare open my eyes to peek. He really was the most extraordinarily beautiful male. The firelight only served to highlight the deep cut of his cheekbones, the fine sculpted shape of his top lip and the beauty of his features. I'd finally fallen asleep myself, aware that our hands were mere inches apart.

So why, if I'd fallen asleep that way, was I currently looking at the back of Sophia's head? I sat up and rubbed my eyes, trying to get a measure of where everyone was in the dark. The only other person awake was Tristam and Sophia's camerawoman who jumped up, pulling her camera to her shoulder ready to film at the first hint of anything exciting. I gave a quick yawn, and sensing that I wasn't going to do anything of interest, after all; she put her camera back down and slouched back against the wall of the cave.

Orin hadn't moved from last night, though he'd turned in his sleep. I glanced over at Tristam, wondering if we were all so cramped up because the cave was smaller than I'd remembered. But no, on Tristam's other side was a space big enough for two or more people if needed. Which begged the question, why was Sophia squashed between Tristam and me? I had a feeling it had nothing to with wanting to cuddle me in the night. She must have woken up in the night, seen how close Tristam and I were and squeezed herself between us, creating an FFR contestant sandwich.

"We should probably head off."

I jumped at Orin's voice. I'd thought I was the only one awake. He was watching me in the low light. I wondered, guiltily, if he could sense the direction of my thoughts.

"Shouldn't we at least wake them?" I whispered.

"Nope," Orin replied with no follow-up explanation. He stood and headed to the mouth of the cave, nudging the sleeping Ben lightly with his foot as he passed.

"But..." I hissed.

He turned and held his forefinger to his lips. Walking back to me and bending his knees until he was at my level, he spoke in a low voice. "May I remind you that there are at least two teams in front of us, possibly more. If we stay here and let these two know we're leaving, they'll want to come with us, and if that happens, we may as well count ourselves out. Besides, I can't bear to spend another minute in pretty boy's company. The guy makes me sick."

I fingered the pendant in my pocket and stood up. The blanket fell to my feet, and I left it there. It would come in handy in the future, but it wasn't mine to take. With a great deal of regret, I followed Orin out of the cave.

"This way." Orin pointed to a field in the distance. Beyond it was the base of Emerald Mountain, rising majestically into the gray dawn.

My mind wandered as we trudged through the thick grass, caught up on other things. Well, one other thing—Tristam. He'd singled me out. Not his own partner, but me. At any point, he could have given the pendant to Sophia, but he hadn't. He'd given it to me. He wanted me to be safe. That thought bubbled up to the surface, but it was what had happened just afterward that filled my mind. I'd been so surprised by the heat of his lips on my cheek that I'd just stood there in stunned silence.

What would he think when he awoke to find us gone? I'd wanted to stay, at least until he was awake so I could say something to him. Not that I knew what. Something. Just leaving without a goodbye or some acknowledgment of what he'd done for me felt unnecessarily rude.

I was so caught up on my own thoughts that I didn't notice the log in the tall grass. It caught my foot and sent me tumbling to the ground. Orin didn't even break his stride to come to my rescue. To be fair, he probably hadn't even noticed I'd fallen. I rubbed my leg and looked crossly at the log. Except it wasn't a log at all. Logs don't have red hair for a start.

"Zee!" I screamed, pulling myself up from where I'd landed on the ground. Her mouth was open and her eyes, devoid of any spark of life, gazed unseeing into the sky.

"No, no, no," I breathed as I bent forward, hovering my ear close above her lips, praying for some sign of life. But I already knew what I'd hear. Still silence. Judging by the state of her body, she'd been dead for at least a few hours, if not closer to a full day. No one could have survived the injuries she had, human or fae. Her upper half was normal, but her legs and hips had been crushed.

Sorrow ripped through me with a fierceness that took my breath away. A sob broke from me, and I pulled her head to my chest, as the tears began to fall. I'd not known her long, and we'd not had much of a chance to bond, but she had been kind to me when she didn't have to be.

Anger curled through me, mingling with the despair. Whatever happened to her could have happened to any one of us. The studios, the Faerie king, all of them were responsible for this, and what for? She'd died in this stinking cesspit of a kingdom just so some bored housewives had something to watch on TV every night and so fat cat studio execs could get even fatter. I didn't know how she died, but I knew she deserved better than this. They hadn't even had the decency to move her body.

"What are you doing...What the..." Orin must have heard me shouting Zee's name out because he appeared behind me.

"She's dead," I sobbed, my tears running free. I'd made a pact with myself that I'd not show emotion, not cry in Faerwild, and I was breaking that pact in the most public way.

But in this moment, I really couldn't care less. Zee's death affected me on a personal level. The least I could give her was a moment of realness in this fake reality show nightmare.

"Where's the other one?" Orin growled, checking the grass around Zee's body.

Genevieve! I'd not thought of her, I'd been too caught up in Zee. But if Zee was here, where was Genevieve?

"Found her," Orin said staring down at something about fifteen feet away from where I sat. His voice was flat. "Jacq...I don't think you should come over here."

Ben rushed over, his camera ready to film, but he stopped short suddenly, his hand flying to his mouth. As I watched, he turned and retched. Orin and I hadn't eaten breakfast, but Ben had a full supply of food in his pack. Whatever he'd consumed that morning came back up, splattering into the grass.

I looked up, wondering if I was being filmed right now. Ben certainly wasn't doing it, but that didn't mean there weren't other secret cameras hidden nearby. This place was full of them.

"You should have taken their bodies," I shouted up into the air. "You can't leave them like this."

I felt a warm hand on my shoulder. I didn't need to look back to know it was Orin.

"I'm sorry Jacq, but we need to leave," he said with an air of urgency. "There's nothing we can do for them, but whatever flattened them could still be out there. We need to get out of this field and quickly. Here, take this." He threw something by my side, and I recognized it as Genevieve's pack.

Lowering Zee's head back to the ground, I picked up the pack as Orin took Zee's. He was right. However much I wanted to stay with Zee and Genevieve, the thing that had killed them was still out there. I didn't want to hang around to find out what it was.

But I couldn't leave them here. I didn't know where their cameraperson was, or if someone was being sent to collect them, but whatever the hell was going on, it was taking too long. A bolt of inspiration struck me.

Pulling the ring from Zee's hand, I pressed the button inside, but nothing happened. There was no flash of light or any other magic I could see. Why wasn't it working?

Without asking Orin's opinion, I turned to Ben, who had recovered, and was filming us once again. "Zee's ring has malfunctioned. I am summoning the FFR officials on her behalf. We do not need extraction."

"Jacq, n—" Orin said, but it was too late.

I twisted the ring on my own finger, pulled it loose, and jabbed the small button inside.

Almost immediately, purple light shot up into the air. It would be seen for miles around.

"What have you done?" he screamed, reaching for the ring, but it was too late. Like it had with Yael and Duncan, a portal opened in the sky, and two faeries in FFR uniforms flew through.

Throwing the ring at Zee's body where it glowed bright purple, I grabbed Orin's hand and tried to pull him away from it as fast as I could.

"Stop," Orin commanded, refusing to be towed away. "Why are you even trying to run? We're disqualified! What the hell, Jacq!"

Instead of answering him, I turned to Ben and his camera and the two FFR officials.

"I told you, we don't need extraction. We're not in danger. I don't want to leave the race," I stated as plainly as possible. "I used the ring so you would pick up Gen and Zee. I couldn't just leave them. It's not right."

Tears rolled down my face, the taste of salt sharp on my lips. "Gen and Zee were good people. They deserved more than this and you…" not sure if I was jabbing my angry finger at the faeries, the camera, the world… "You left them there. Left their bodies to rot. Now you can take them home where they belong. To their families. I used the ring for them, not for us."

The two faeries exchanged quiet words, and then one held up a finger to his ear, to an earpiece tucked inside his pointed ear. He was listening to instructions. Then he nodded.

"The producers would like me to relate that you have not been disqualified. We understand that the use of the ring was not for purposes of extraction."

Relief welled in me.

"You will not be given a new emergency ring. Each competitor is entitled to one."

I blinked at that before my eyes narrowed. Assholes. I opened my mouth to protest when Orin's hand closed around mine. "It's fine, we only need one. I have mine." He tugged me back towards the mountain behind us. "Let's go before they change their minds," he hissed.

"You'll take their bodies?" I called, letting him drag me away.

The faerie nodded, and I knew it was as good as I was going to get. We took off across the field, Ben huffing behind us.

"Damn it, Jacq," Orin panted. "Never do something like that again. I get that you have a hero complex or something, but they were already gone. You didn't help, and you almost got us kicked out of the race."

My words were kindling to the fury that was already building within me at FFR's treatment of Gen and Zee. "Sorry my hero complex got in the way of your...anti-hero complex."

"That's not a thing," Orin glared sideways at me.

"Well, I don't know what to call it when a person refuses to lift a finger to help anyone but themselves."

"A healthy sense of self-preservation? Besides, if you wanted to use a ring, why not use theirs?"

"I did. I tried Zee's, and nothing happened. I didn't use mine lightly."

That shut him up. "Why didn't it work?"

"If it had worked in the first place they'd probably be alive right now. Something is going on, and I think the people running the FFR are in on it."

Orin goggled at me. "You think they let them die purposely?"

"I don't know, Orin," I slowed to a walk, panting. "I just know two smart competitors are dead, and it doesn't make a lick of sense."

Orin huffed and threw Zee's pack to the ground. He knelt down and unzipped the bag. "I want to see what we have in those packs. We need food. Water."

It felt wrong to open Genevieve's pack, but I had to remind myself that it would be no use to her now. The stuff inside might save our lives.

Orin emptied the contents of Zee's bag onto the ground, and I followed suit, pouring everything belonging to Genevieve on top. There wasn't much, but some of it would come in handy. A bit of food, a knife, a crossbow, some arrows, some sort of magic dust. And a letter.

The food—just a couple of bags of nuts and some browning apple slices—I doled out between Orin and me.

"I can shoot," I said, picking the crossbow up in limp fingers. The image of Zee's vacant eyes, the purple of her tattoos against unnaturally pale skin flashed in my mind, and my stomach roiled.

"Take it," Orin said, passing me the arrows still in their quiver. "I'll take the magic dust and the knife." He took both and put them back in Zee's pack.

"What about this?" I picked up the letter. It seemed a shame to leave it behind. What if it was the last correspondence Genevieve or Zee ever received? It could be a letter full of *I love you's* from one of their mothers. It could be a love letter, though I didn't know Genevieve or Zee well enough to know if either had a significant other at home. My heart broke as I thought of their families waking up to the news that they'd never see their daughters again.

I picked the letter up to shove it back in Gen's pack when the handwriting stopped me in my tracks. Those curls on the letters. Cheerful and perky. Surely...no. My hands felt numb as I fumbled the letter out of its envelope. It was folded in the shape of a flower. My eyes widened in shock as all the air in my lungs seemed to leave me. This letter was from my sister.

23

The letter shook in my hands like a leaf in a gale. I wanted to stroke the paper, to touch something my sister's hands had touched. This letter was proof my sister was alive. Proof that she was here. In an instant, my relief bloomed into hurt. If she could send a letter over the Hedge to Gen, then why hadn't she sent one to me? To my parents...just to let us know that she was all right? I almost ripped the thick paper as I unfolded the flower to read what was inside.

My eager eyes gobbled up the words, trying to make sense of the missive. It was clear they were familiar, that they'd been corresponding, for there weas no "How are you" or catching up. Cass had dived right in, her normally sweet handwriting, filled with curls and flourishes, seemed abrupt and hurried.

Gen-

Double bad news. We didn't find a MED in Caerleon. Doesn't mean it's not there. Worse, there's been a break-in at HQ. We've had to move. It means you could be compromised. We know the Brotherhood has infiltrated the FFR. Be careful.

-Cass

The words chilled me to my core even as the questions burned within me. What the hell was a MED? Whose HQ? Who was Cass with? Was she free? The letter didn't sound as if she had been taken or was being held against her will. But if she was free...then why had she stayed away? And the Brotherhood...That was what I'd heard Patricia talking about with Niall back at the start of the race. Who were they and what did Patricia and Niall have to do with my sister?

There was something sinister going on, and I didn't like it. Not one bit. This just compounded my thought that Genevieve and Zee's deaths weren't accidental.

"You look like you've seen a ghost," Orin said, crouching down behind me and reading over my shoulder.

For once, his presence didn't bother me—he grounded me, tying me back to this place. I opened my mouth to explain when Ben's blinking light entered my vision. I didn't know who they were trying to stop, but it probably wouldn't help Cass's cause if I outed her on worldwide television. I quickly folded the letter and shoved it back in the envelope. "Just some private letter." If I could get Orin alone without Ben's blinking eye, I'd tell him. Maybe he'd know some-thing. "I wish I could tell where it came from. Maybe we could notify them about Gen."

Orin took the envelope from me, turning it over. "It's from Elfame." He pointed at a stamp of a twisting current of wind. "It's the sign of the Slyph Couriers. They deliver mail and packages throughout Faerwild."

"So the letter came from here," I said.

"Yes. They're based in Elfame, though. The writer's probably there."

I surged to my feet. "Let's go," I said.

Orin stood, crossing his arms before him. "What? To Elfame?"

"Yes, come on!"

"Jacq. What is going on with you? We need to get to the Emerald Mountain. We need to finish the trial. Remember? We both worked hard to be here." His eyes flicked to Ben. "We both have reasons."

But my reason was to find Cass, and now I'd found her. I needed to get to her. I wanted to scream it at him, to make him understand. But...I faltered. "How many people live in Elfame?" I asked.

"People? Not many."

I rolled my eyes. "Faeries. Magical creatures. You know what I mean."

"Several hundred thousand, I think."

I blanched. The letter didn't have a return address on it. Looking for Cass would be like trying to find a needle in a haystack. Especially if she didn't want to be found. Which it seemed possible she didn't. The Faerie king's boon was still my best chance of finding her. I couldn't leave. I needed to finish this race.

"Okay," I said, shoving the letter in Gen's pack and throwing it over my shoulder. "Let's finish this."

"You mean this trial. You realize there are still two more trials to go before the race is over?"

I hissed, motioning him forward. "Yes, yes. Let's just get to the checkpoint and fight whatever monster they throw at us."

"The sword seems to indicate it's a dragon."

I closed my eyes, fighting my frustration. I didn't have time to banter with Orin. I didn't have time for this damn race. Now that I knew Cass was alive and here, it was all I could think of. The urge to move, to run, to find her was overwhelming. "Lead the way," I said through gritted teeth.

Orin forged ahead.

We trekked up the side of the mountain as the tall grass gave way to rocks and scree fields. My legs burned with the effort of the ascent, even as my stomach growled. I was weak with hunger, my muscles crying out for fuel. My mind, which normally settled into a Zen-like state when I exerted myself, refused to be silent, spinning in circles over Cass's sudden return to my life, over Genevieve's death. How long had the two girls been writing to each other? Had Gen known all along where Cass was, even as she sat at our kitchen table and tearfully told the police she'd seen nothing? I wanted nothing more than to ask her. But she was dead, along with whatever answers she held.

Orin stopped for a moment, pulling a canteen from Zee's pack. He took a swig and passed it to me. The water was warm and metallic tasting. I longed for a crisp cold drink of pure water. Or a beer. God, a cold beer sounded nice right about now.

"Do you know where we're going?" I asked, more grumpily than was necessary. "Or are we just traipsing up the hill, hoping we stumble upon something?"

Orin pointed at a jagged outcropping of rock on the mountain face above us. It looked far, though I had lost my sense of distance in this monotonous landscape of rock and sky. "We'll find it up there."

I nodded wearily, too tired to question him. If we didn't find it there, I thought I'd just curl up and die. My head was pounding, and my thoughts felt fuzzy. "Do we have any more food?" I asked.

He shook his head. "Come on," he grabbed my hand and

pulled me forward. "There will be a feast at the end of this trial. We'll have a day of rest, with real beds and everything."

"Real beds," I moaned. "Feast."

"I want buttermilk pancakes with maple syrup and berries and enough whipped cream to drown in," Orin said, his eyes fixed before him.

"They have pancakes in Faerwild?" I asked.

"We're not complete savages," he looked sideways at me.

"Silly me," I said. "I'm sure the Red Caps enjoy a side of waffles with their meal of human flesh."

"Ok well, some faeries are savages. Not me."

That was becoming clear to me in a way that made me uneasy. I wasn't sure at what point it had shifted, but Orin was no longer my enemy. I no longer loathed him or feared him. I was contemplating this strange turn of events when a shadow passed above us.

I looked up wearily, expecting to see a cloud passing over the sun. What I saw was a very large, very huge red dragon. Headed directly for us.

"Orin," I screamed as the beast dipped low, its talons outstretched towards us. I barreled into Orin, knocking him down towards the rocky ground, but the dragon was too fast. Those wicked talons, as long as my forearms, closed around us and hoisted us up into the air.

I'm not proud of the bloodcurdling scream that exploded from me, but you try getting picked up by a mother-effing dragon and see if you keep your cool.

Orin and I were sandwiched together between the creature's talons, myself on top of him, Orin struggling beneath me. "Do...something..." I gasped, as Orin pulled one hand free to perform a spell.

But the dragon was winging towards the sky, bearing us higher and higher into the air. "I'm afraid...it'll drop us," he groaned, as I accidentally elbowed him in the side trying to better secure my own hold. Because now I was getting less afraid of being in the dragon's talons, and starting to worry about what would happen if we *fell out*. My eyes opened wide as realization crashed into me. "Oh god," I said, meeting Orin's wide black eyes. "Gen. Zee. Crushed in the middle of a field..."

The dragon was swooping over the field below its mountain, banking around.

"It's going to drop us," Orin whispered, the fear evident in his voice. He was afraid of heights, and at this point, I could hardly blame him.

"Do you know a flying spell?" I asked desperately.

"No—" Orin began, but the rest of his answer was lost to the wind. For the dragon opened its claws and released us into the wide blue sky.

24

My body dropped into freefall. The wind howled past my ears as my stomach lurched upwards. I tried to grab hold of Orin, though with him falling at roughly the same speed as me, it was a pointless endeavor.

My mind raced for some way out of this even as I realized that there was none. I was going to die. I was going to be flattened on the ground like the pancakes we'd been talking about only moments before, whether I held Orin's hand or not. I instinctively felt for the ring on my finger. The ring that would get us out of this, but it was already gone. I'd used the only chance of survival available to me. I screamed at Orin to use his, but his eyes were clenched shut, and the deafening wind that flew past us gobbled up my words. He was petrified with panic—past the point of reason.

And yet, something spurred me on, urged me to reach him. I realized what it was in a flash. I didn't want to die alone. And so, in my final moments, as the ground rushed up to meet us, my hand sought his. As we made contact and our fingers entwined, it became apparent that even his magic could not save us. I tried to scream at him to use the ring, but my words were whipped from me. I couldn't reach his other hand with the ring.

Something around my neck freed itself from my jacket and whipped me in my face. Tristam's necklace. A singular lance of hope shot through me. He'd told me to use it in an emergency. With the ground racing up to meet us, I figured this constituted an emergency. Clasping my hand around the pendant, with the last breath I was ever going to take, I screamed out the word Tristam had taught me and prayed I'd get it right.

"Diogelwch!"

I closed my eyes mere feet from the ground and waited for either the quickness of death or a miracle. When the inevitable crash didn't come, and the howling wind turned into an eerie silence, I opened my eyes. Below me was a dark stretch of dirt. Before my senses told me I was suspended in mid-air, the magic or whatever it was that was holding me up faded, and both Orin and I fell the couple of feet to the ground with a lurch.

I groaned, laying there for a moment, letting my hammering heart slow.

"What the..." Orin pulled his hand from mine and used it to dust himself off. The landing had been much softer than it would have been without Tristam's talisman, but it still smarted as I turned around and brought myself into a sitting position.

I was about to tell Orin, with great glee, that Tristam had been the one to save us when I realized we weren't exactly where I expected us to be. I'd thought we would land directly under where the dragon had dropped us. My assumption was that the talisman had slowed our descent and softened our impact. That assumption was very clearly wrong. For I was now looking at four dark walls and a dark ceiling above us.

"What the hell happened? I didn't do this," Orin said with a perplexed expression on his face. He gazed at his hands as though they had somehow produced magic without his commanding them to.

"I know. It wasn't you." I put my hand on his and lowered it so he'd concentrate on me and what I had to say. Now, if only I could figure out what that was. Looking around, we were in a dark cave with a tunnel leading off into pitch blackness. The only illumination was a very faint blue light that had no discernible source. It made Orin look even paler than he usually did and his black hair was highlighted with blue. "I brought us here."

"I'll forgo the *how* for now," he said, glancing around him, "and move straight onto the *why*...and for that matter the *where*. Where exactly are we?"

I sighed, knowing I'd have to come clean about Tristam and the talisman. And how...it now seemed that the talisman was not in fact designed to save me. But to trap me. Embarrassment heated my face. Like a lovesick little puppy I'd fallen for his pretty face and believed every word he said. Orin was going to have a field day when I told him.

"I don't know where we are. To be honest, I suspect wherever it is, it's not going to be easy to get out of. I didn't actually bring us here on purpose. I was trying to save our lives...with this." I pulled the chain out from around my neck and held the pendant up in the pale light so Orin could get a good look at it.

"That's the royal crest," he said, pulling the chain from between my fingers and examining it more closely. "Where did you get this fro...Oh, you didn't?"

My stomach churned as he looked back up at me. "Tristam gave this to you, didn't he? And you accepted it?"

I shifted uncomfortably on my feet. "In my defense, it did just save our lives. Without it, we'd be nothing more than pulp in a field somewhere."

"Granted, but we're not really in a much better situation now, are we?"

"We're alive," I huffed. "I'd say that's moderately better than being dead."

Orin shrugged his shoulders and took off down the tunnel. I raced after him before he was swallowed up entirely by the darkness.

I could hear him mumbling to himself under his breath the whole way up the tunnel. Every so often I'd catch the odd word, like *idiot* or *pathetic.*

"If you've got something to say, you may as well come out with it," I huffed as we entered another cave. This one was equally nondescript as the first, but it had three other tunnels shooting off from it.

"I cannot believe you trusted him," Orin said darkly. "He's our competition! And the king's son! After I told you..." he trailed off, looking around, and then his eyes widened. We both seemed to realize at the same time that Ben wasn't in here with us. No cameras.

Orin went on. "After I told you about what the king did to my family. The Obanstones care only for themselves. No one else. Especially not mortals."

"Left or right?" I asked, unsuccessfully trying to keep his words from needling me. I was a mortal. As useless as an insect to faeries.

"Let's go straight on," he replied, of course, to be difficult. I huffed and skirted around Orin, taking the path in the middle. Seconds later, he'd caught up with me.

"What was it about him that made you fall for his tricks? His golden flyaway hair? His masculine pout? His delectable eyes?"

"Sounds like you're the one who's mooning over him, not me," I snapped. "I thought he was trying to help." I could hardly admit I'd developed a crush on him. That's exactly what Orin wanted to hear...or not hear. Who knew?

"Well, thanks to your pretty boy, we are stuck in this hole, and I for one, don't see a way out."

"Drop it," I cautioned. "I was wrong to trust him."

"Yes, you were. Never trust a faerie!"

"I was wrong to trust him," I repeated, "but without his talisman we'd both be dead and unable to continue this argument. So let's get over it and find the way out." My angry words echoed as we came upon another cave. Like the last one, it had four exits including the one we'd just come from.

Without bothering to ask Orin, I stalked through it and picked the tunnel straight ahead, as we'd had done the last time.

We walked for miles, always taking the middle tunnel. Pain shot through my feet with each step and my stomach was once again growling for food.

"There's something wrong here," Orin said as we once again came to a crossroads. "Every cave but the first has had four points of entry or exit whichever way you look at it."

"So?" I asked. "I figure if we go in a straight line, we'll eventually find a way out. The ground beneath us is flat, so it's not like we're going deeper into the earth."

Orin shook his head. "I'm not so sure. Pass me your pack."

"Why?"

"Never mind. Mine will do just as well." He pulled his

backpack from his shoulders and dropped it to the floor. "Let's go."

"You're leaving it behind?" I asked, rushing to catch up with him as he made his way up the central tunnel.

"I really hope I'm wrong," he replied cryptically. "If I am, I'll go back for it, but if I'm right, which I hope I'm not, then..." He stopped mid-sentence as we came upon another cave. There, right in the center was a backpack. Orin's backpack.

Orin let out a roar of frustration before shouting out a list of expletives that almost certainly would have been bleeped out of the show if Ben was still filming us. "This isn't a normal cave system. There is a reality-bending spell on it."

"A what?" I asked confused.

He handed me his backpack. "Here, let me show you. Stay exactly where you are. I'll be right back." As he walked away from me, leaving me alone in the cave, a sense of foreboding crept over me. For a brief second, I began to panic that he'd left me and when I felt a tap on my shoulder from behind I nearly jumped right out of my skin.

"It's me," Orin said as I tried to get my breathing under control.

We'd been walking for hours, and effectively, we'd barely moved at all. Frustration bubbled up as I realized I was just as far away from Cass as I'd ever been. I'd felt so close to getting to her just a couple of hours before, but now here I was trapped in the cave of nightmares with Orin.

"I'm never going to see her again am I?"

"I don't know," replied Orin, his voice sounding much lower than usual.

"Now, you decide to be honest! When I want you to lie to me and tell me everything is going to be okay."

"I don't know that everything is going to be all right, and I don't see any sense in pandering to your fear and telling you otherwise. I don't even know if we'll get out of this place, and I don't know if I'll ever be able to help my parents and don't know why I entered this godforsaken race in the first place." He kicked the dirt beneath his feet leaving a mark on the floor. It gave me an idea.

"Stop moping and follow me," I said, a bit harshly, as it had been me that had started the moping in the first place. "I have an idea."

Where Orin had kicked a line in the dirt, I used the tip of my shoe to put another line through it, making it into a cross. Instead of going straight forward, I took Orin's hand in mine and took the left-hand tunnel. As I had hoped, the next cave we came to had no mark on the ground.

"There is a way out of this place after all. We just need to figure it out." In this cave, I drew a circle in the dirt and took one of the tunnels which lead us right back to itself. Without stopping, we took another until we came to a cave with no markings.

With trial and error, we wove our way through the strange cave, making different markings each time we entered a new cave. Some of the caves took three attempts before we entered a new one, but if we stuck to the plan, we'd find a way out eventually...in theory.

Hours later, I was beginning to think that maybe I was wrong and there was an endless supply of these virgin caves. Maybe this whole place was designed to give you false hope and keep you going until the despair finally kicked in, leaving you wondering if you should just fall to the floor and give up entirely. I had it in the back of my mind to articulate this to Orin for a while, but then a little voice in my head told me if I gave up now, I'd never know if the exit was in the next cave.

But even my voice of hope left me when, after hours and hours and hours of walking we entered a cave with a cross. It was the cross we'd drawn with our feet. We'd walked for what felt like forever only to come round in a circle.

I collapsed to the floor in despair and let my head fall into my hands. If Tristam was here right now, I'd happily rip his gorgeous head off his shoulders and drop kick it down a tunnel. I'd do it with a smile on my face too. At least, that would make my death that bit more palatable, for that's what Orin and I were facing.

Tristam's pendant had taken away our quick, painless death and replaced it with one that would be long and drawn out as dehydration overcame us.

"Will you be quiet," hissed Orin, pulling his forefinger to his lips. I hadn't even been aware I was making any noise... not unless I'd been expressing my thoughts out loud.

"I can hear something."

I froze. He was right. There was a voice calling out to us in soft feminine tones. We weren't here alone after all. There was someone down here. And it knew our names.

25

I scrambled to my feet, grabbing a sharp rock in my sweaty palm. "What is that?" I whispered.

Orin's face was pale in the dim light. "I don't know."

"What kind of faeries live in caves?"

He shook his head. "Not ones that you want to encounter." He took a step forward as the lilting voice called out, "Orin, come here, Orin."

I grabbed his bicep and hauled him back. "Where the hell do you think you're going?"

He didn't look at me, his eyes fixed ahead. "I'm going to check it out."

"Going towards the mysterious, creepy monster voice? I don't think so," I said, trying to keep him beside me as he pulled forward again. Did this creature have some sort of hold over him?

But he turned back to me, and his dark eyes were clear. "Whatever that is may know the way out of here. We have to try."

"It could be dangerous," I hissed. "Attack us." The

memory of the Red Cap biting into Duncan's leg with razor teeth filled my mind.

"Feel free to slowly starve to death in this circular hell cave, but I'm going to check it out." He pulled his arm from my grip and stalked forward, through the tunnel toward where the voice was floating from.

I bit my lip, indecision warring at me. I felt like I was in the worst kind of choose-your-own-adventure. Whatever page I turned to, I would end up dead. The End. I shook my head, hurrying after Orin. When had I become such a scaredy-cat? I chided myself. I used to be fearless. This place hadn't taken that from me completely, had it?

The tunnel opened into a cave unlike any we'd been in before. It had a soaring ceiling that glittered with clear crystals and winked with more of the faint blue light. Instead of the packed dirt and rock we'd been walking over, this huge cavern was covered with dark, cool water, a massive subterranean lake. Across the cavern was a tinkling river pouring sparkling water out of a dark recess in the wall. And next to it was the source of the voice. A woman.

Orin was picking his way around the stones that skirted the lake, heading towards the woman. She stood with a pitcher on her hip and called out again. "Come, Jacqueline," she said, motioning gracefully with a hand.

The hairs on the back of my neck rose, but I followed Orin. As I approached, I got a better view of our hostess. She was exquisitely beautiful, with long blonde hair that flowed almost to her waist. That would be a bitch to brush through, I thought. Her creamy, flawless skin was pale and almost glowed in the eerie light of the cave. She wore a dress that looked like spun silk, in the color of the sky on a cool winter's day. Her appearance, though lovely, didn't set me at ease. It was always the pretty girls in the stories who had sharp teeth and swallowed you whole as soon as your back was turned. I wasn't about to let that happen.

"Orin Treebaum," the woman-faerie-creature said. "Welcome to my cave." She set down her pitcher and took his hand. Thoughts of the other creatures that had already tried to mislead us entered my head. Orin had been the one to warn me against them, so why was he giving her his hand? It made no sense. I resisted shouting at him not to touch her, but thankfully, nothing seemed to happen when they touched.

"How do you know us?" Orin asked.

"This is my home," she said. "It has no secrets from me."

"You...live here?" I asked, looking around. Seemed kinda lonely. And depressing.

She inclined her head towards me, a smile twitching on those perfect plush lips. "I am a xana. Caves such as this one give us life. Imbue us with their magic. And so we act as guardians."

"A xana?" I asked. Orin exchanged a glance with me, but his expression was unreadable. He recognized the term, but I wasn't sure if he was relieved or struck with terror. "Do you have anything to do with the spell back there?" I asked. "The one turning us around in circles?"

She shook her head. "Such mischievous magic is not mine. That cave is not a part of my home, for I would not have allowed such an enchantment. But I heard your voices, and so I opened a passage here so we could speak."

"So, we're out of the loop?" I asked, with hope. "Can we get to the surface from here?"

She wrinkled her perfect brow. "But why would you want to? Everything a person needs is here."

"Everything a xana needs, perhaps," Orin said gently. "But not a human. Or a faerie. We need food. And sunlight."

She nodded slowly. "Yes, that does make sense."

"Can you help us get out of here?" I asked, and Orin shot me a dirty look. "Not...that it's not lovely here...in your cave. But we...we have important tasks to complete."

One slender eyebrow rose. "A quest? You are adventurers on a quest?" She seemed delighted at the prospect.

"Yes," Orin said. "A very important quest that we must complete or lives will be lost. Please, my lady. We are at your mercy."

I wanted to snort. That was laying it on a little thick, but the xana seemed to eat it up. She clapped her hands. "If I am to aid you..."—she drew a finger to her lip, considering—"you must grant me a token...or a boon. Yes, that is the way of quests."

Orin and I frowned at each other. She wanted something? I wracked my brain, and then a thought occurred to me. I pulled Tristam's necklace out of my pocket and held it out to her. "This necklace was given to me by the crown prince of all of Faerwild. As a sign of his affection. It has great power. But I shall give it to you, in exchange for your aid."

The xana flowed towards me, taking the necklace reverently. Up close, she was even more beautiful, her irises like refracted crystals, her eyelashes long and fair. The girl didn't even need mascara with those lashes, I thought to myself darkly. No wonder Orin was lapping this up.

The xana fixed the necklace around her throat and turned to Orin. "And what boon shall you give me, brave Orin?"

Orin was fishing in his pockets. I could see him considering what he had. The dragon sword. We really needed that. I shook my head to him. He needed to come up with something else.

"Might I suggest..." the xana said coyly, stepping up to him, "a kiss?"

Orin's dark eyebrows flew skyward, and when he spoke, his voice cracked. "You..." he cleared his throat. "You would take that? As payment?"

"It has been long since I have enjoyed the kiss of such a young, virile, faerie male. I would," she said, her fingers playing with the button on the front of his shirt.

Orin looked at me, his eyes a question I didn't fully understand, so I couldn't answer. There was no way he was going to do it. Not Orin. I couldn't imagine him kissing anyone. I expected to see his face color at the suggestion, but it was I who was surprised as he leaned down and kissed her.

I'm not sure what I was expecting. Her arms to turn to tentacles, her face into a sucking maw that would swallow him up. Well, that didn't happen. But I *also* didn't expect them to wrap their arms around each other, Orin taking her head with his hand as he deepened the kiss, as they pressed against each other. Jesus, he was really going to town!

I was frozen to the spot, unable to look away, unable to combat the uncomfortable whirlwind of emotions that were rushing up to meet me. And the heat that washed over me, pooling deep in my core at the sight of Orin literally ravishing the xana—his lips and hands navigating her form with expert attention. The xana moaned softly and my face flushed red as I realized what I was feeling. Oh god. Jealousy. Surely not. Not for Orin.

I cleared my throat loudly, shoving the unwelcome realization down ruthlessly. It wasn't Orin I wanted. I just hadn't been kissed by anyone like that in a long time. *Maybe ever*, a voice in my head said, and I swatted at it.

Orin and the xana were untwining from each other, and

he wiped his mouth, unable to keep a languid smile from creeping onto his face. I wanted to smack it off. I wanted to punch him. I wanted to punch him right in his smug perfect face. If I didn't want to get out of this damn cave more, I might just have done it.

"Well," the xana smoothed her hair, adjusting her gown. She looked like the cat who had just eaten the canary. "That was quite a boon. More, I think, than is necessary in exchange for my aid." She crossed a few stones and began picking her way across stepping stones through the babbling river. "Come," she said.

Orin and I fell into step behind her, and I shot him my most powerful scowl. It did not feel up to the task.

"What?" He shrugged, still wearing that incorrigible grin. "Just doing what's necessary for the team."

I twisted a fake smile at him, narrowing my eyes. "Your sacrifice is noted."

The xana stopped and bent over, reaching into the water. When she stood, she turned and held out a tiny crystal vial to Orin. "This is a love potion. A gift from me, in thanks for your kiss. Though a male with as passionate a soul as yours need no potion, it is all I have to give. Perhaps it will serve you along your journey."

"The potion, and the way out?" I clarified. "Right? You can get us out of here, too?"

Orin shot me a look. "Thank you, beautiful xana. I shall not forget you or your generosity."

"Nor I," she murmured, looking him up and down. I glanced away in mortification. Get a room, lady!

But she motioned forward, towards a dark opening in the cave beyond the stream. "Follow the lights. They will lead you home."

26

Orin leaned over and took the xana's hand, kissing it lightly the way any gentleman would in a black and white movie.

At least it was like an old movie until I nudged past him and accidentally sent him splashing into the shallows of the water.

"Oops," I said as he trudged back to the rocks, his dark eyes glittering furiously. "My bad!"

Of course, the xana just had to help, pulling him out of the water and using her magic to drain the water from his pants and boots. Did she want another boon for that too?

"You pushed me on purpose!" Orin snarled as we left the crystal cave and the xana behind.

"I can't imagine what you're talking about."

Orin strode past me, nearly knocking me over in the narrow tunnel. "Oops."

I guess I deserved that. I rubbed my arm where he'd barged past and followed him out into the open air.

The pair of us stood, our hair fluttering in the wind that had picked up during our time in the cave. We were undoubtedly on the same mountain we'd been climbing before I invoked Tristam's stupid talisman, but judging by the view, we'd walked right beneath the mountain and were now on the other side.

Elfame was way behind us now, and even though we were closer to the end of this stupid race, I felt like I was heading further and further away from the reason I'd come here in the first place...Cass.

"Now what?" I asked, looking out into the distance. The light was fading, and all I could see was miles and miles of meadows ahead of us. There was no sign of the others still left in the race, no campfires, nothing. I wondered where they all were. Were they all done? Had we lost this trial?

"We still have to get the next clue from the dragon."

Right. The damn dragon. Funnily enough, my mind had been so filled with endless caves and kisses that lasted too long that I had forgotten the dragon. On second thought, I'd rather think of the dragon than that painfully long kiss I'd been forced to watch.

"What?" Orin said, pulling me out of my thoughts.

"What what?"

"You said you'd rather think of a dragon."

Crap. I'd been thinking aloud again. Hopefully, he'd not heard the last part of that thought. "Yeah, dragon," I mumbled, trying to sound like I knew what I was talking about. "Let's go kick its ass."

"Hmm," Orin replied, following my purposeful walk out from the mouth of the cave and up the mountain. "That's not what it sounded like to me."

Thankfully, the darkness of the evening hid my reddening cheeks. Damned if I knew what was going on with me. It must be something to do with all the magic fizzing about. It was bound to do something to the mind if one was surrounded by enough of it.

Despite my determined pace, climbing the mountain was harder than I thought it would be. The wind was much colder up here, and I didn't have the right gear for the temperature. I had to resist the urge to ask Orin for help. After the display he'd just put on, I was in no mood to ask him for anything.

"Slow down!" I heard him panting behind me. "This is exhausting."

"Okay," I yelled, picking up the pace. He could do with a bit of exercise. It would help him get thoughts of xanas out of his tiny brain.

I felt his hand on my shoulder, forcing me to stop and turn around. "Will you slow down! I just told you I was exhausted."

"Did you?" I asked, trying to school my features into an innocent expression. "I didn't hear you in all this wind."

Okay, I was being a bitch, and both of us knew it, but I was annoyed with him. Now, if only I could articulate why I was annoyed, then both of us could be happier. I ignored that little voice in my head that told me that jealousy was my motivation and softened. "I'm sorry. I'll walk slower."

"Good. We still have a dragon to fight after all of this, and I don't want to be half dead when I do it."

He started off again, leaving me stock-still. Thoughts of Zee and Genevieve's flattened mutilated bodies crashed through my brain, and I picked up my pace to keep close to Orin.

I'd not put much thought into fighting any kind of dragon. In the movies, any action scene, especially ones involving dragons, would be filmed using a green screen and CGI. But after our last attempt, I knew we needed to do better. In theory, I knew how to kill a dragon—find the weak points in its scaly hide, right? Avoid the deadly fire, claws, and flailing tail? My stomach flipped. We could do this.

As the thought passed my mind, something dark flew overhead and blocked the moonlight for a few seconds. Grabbing Orin's hand and forgetting the argument between us, I raced up the mountain to the black hole I could just make out above us.

The cave was the only shelter from the dragon I could see, so with every ounce of strength I possessed, I pushed forwards, pulling a wheezing Orin behind me. Once in the cave, I let go of him, dropping my hands to my knees to catch my breath.

"I think we've outrun him," I huffed, my lungs screaming from exertion.

"I think you've brought us into his home," Orin panted back, eyeing up the corner of the cave. I followed his eye line and saw a stack of bones piled up at the edge of the cave. Some of those looked to be human. I'd messed up. I'd messed up big.

"Don't panic," Orin said, coming towards me.

"I'm sorry." I murmured. I'd been so caught up in everything, I'd made a ghastly mistake. It was so stupid. I cursed myself for letting my emotions take over and hung my head.

"No time for that," Orin said, his voice unusually tender. He pressed one finger to my chin and gently raised my face until I was eye to eye with him. I could barely see him in the dim light, but I could see enough to know he was worried about me. "We need to fight this thing, but neither of us can do it alone. I have the magic. You have stealth and strength on your side." He handed me the sword and pushed up his sleeves. "Between us, we have a chance to get through this, but we will need to work together. Are you with me?"

I nodded.

As he nodded back, cementing our new pact, the little light in the cave was snuffed out by the shadow of the dragon. Taking a deep breath, I held my hand up in the air. Orin high fived me quietly then turned towards our enemy, falling into a fighting stance. In the movies, this would be the epic end scene where the audience knew the heroes would win but sat on the edge of their seat all the same. I had no such knowledge. There was no script. There was every chance we'd die here.

With a scream that echoed around the cave, I lunged towards the black shape, the sword aloft in my hand. In almost slow motion, the dragon turned its head and blasted fire from its mouth straight towards me. I ducked, but I didn't need to. Orin had performed a spell shielding me from the fire, deflecting it back on the dragon.

The dragon yelped as the full force of its flames hit it in the wing. Giving a huge roar, it turned its attention on Orin.

I thought the force field would protect him too, but the angry dragon burst through it as though it was nothing more than tissue paper. It took me a few seconds to realize what was going on and those few seconds cost us. The dragon lunged at Orin, knocking him off his feet. I heard the sound of bones cracking just half a second before the ear-piercing scream left Orin's mouth.

The dragon had done nothing more than knock him over with its snout, but he'd tumbled the wrong way, breaking something in the process. He was helpless as the dragon opened its mouth, ready to scoop him up for dinner.

With a yell of my own, I raised the sword over my head and ran towards the dragon, ramming it down as hard as I could. With a chink, the sword bounced off its thick leather hide, nearly causing me to drop it as the reverberations shuddered down my body.

"You need magic to make the sword strong enough against dragon skin," Orin shouted. A quick glance over at him showed me he was in agony and in no fit state to help me.

"I can't do magic!" I whispered to myself in a panic as the dragon spun around, no longer interested in Orin. He wanted to play with his food before eating it, it seemed. At least, I could lure it away from Orin. Running outside into the fading light, I felt a blast of hot air burn the hair from my right arm and blister the skin.

"That hurt!" I screamed, turning around to face the dragon.

Its jaws widened as it lumbered towards me.

I could see right down its throat. If I angled the sword just right, towards the soft part of the flesh at the very back of its mouth, I knew I wouldn't need magic. But the rows of razor-sharp teeth heading towards me made me waver. It would take split-second timing and a truckload of luck to kill it before it ripped me to shreds. Magic was my only real option.

I thought about what Tristam had shown me, and then about Orin's story about his father. About making magic his friend. A fluffy little bunny. Gathering up every bit of imagination I could muster, I imagined magic as my own little dragon. Powerful and glowing, ready to face my foe beside me. I had to do this. This couldn't be the end of the road for Orin and me. He needed to free his parents, and I needed to find Cass. I was here in this place, going through this hell, for her. If I didn't embrace magic now, it would all be for nothing. And I'd never see her again. Not to mention turn out as a dragon shish kebab.

I imagined my friendly magical dragon pouring its own power and fire into the sword, promising it belly scratches and treats if it cooperated. And it WORKED. At the very last second, the sword began to glow and instead of aiming for the back of its throat, I sliced upwards, ramming the boiling hot sword right up the dragon's nose.

I don't know who was more shocked by this sudden turn of events—the dragon or me. I'd performed magic. Real magic!

The dragon's slitted eyes widened as it began to scream and flail, its motion wrenching the sword hilt from my hand. Without my weapon or Orin to help me, I could only watch as the large beast swung its head about before falling to the ground with a crash.

I pressed myself against the back of the cave to avoid the dragon's death throes. Its roar of agony reverberated against my eardrums. I ducked behind a cluster of rocks and tripped over a long wooden crate stashed out of the way. I frowned at it. In the low light, I could just make out the faint symbol of a rose and thistle spray painted on it. Somewhere in the back of my mind, I recognized it, but the dragon's flailing razor-sharp claws and thrashing tail were the more pressing issue at the moment.

Finally, the dragon fell still. Its glassy eyes reflected the stars that had appeared in the sky outside the cave. They held no light of their own.

I'd killed it. I'd actually killed it using magic.

A grin split across my face. I wasn't going to let Orin hear the end of this. Not for a long while.

27

As Orin and I stumbled out of the cave, Orin leaning heavily on me to keep weight off his injured ankle, a bright light greeted us. I threw up my arm to shield my eyes and tried to make out what it was.

The blinking red light clued me in. "Jacq?" I heard Ben's worried voice and another that I didn't recognize.

"Ms. Cunningham! Mr. Treebaum!" A fae female in an FFR jumpsuit ran up to us. "Do you need medical attention?" she asked.

"What the hell does it look like?" I snapped. "He's got a broken ankle, and I'm burned half to hell."

"Okay," she said, not flinching at my rudeness. "We'll transport you back to headquarters."

"How—" I started to ask, but she was already grabbing us both and whispering something that sounded a lot like magic. And the next thing I knew, everything went black.

My stomach heaved within me, and my head spun when I opened my eyes back up. The mountain was gone. In its place, was a huge ballroom with a soaring ceiling above us and polished marble floors beneath our dirty boots.

Bright lights and a crowd surrounded us—people were everywhere, clapping and cheering. And cameras. So many cameras.

Orin and I looked at each other in confusion, trying to reconcile the past few moments of dirt and near death with this sudden thrust into the glittering Hollywood light.

Patricia trotted our way with a microphone in hand and five-inch stilettos on her feet.

"Jacq! Orin!" she purred, as I continued to blink. A face in the crowd came into focus in the background. Bubblegum pink hair. Molly. The contestants were here. I scanned the crowd, ignoring Patricia like a buzzing fly. There he was. Blond hair. Perfectly tan face, white teeth flashing in a smile.

"'Scuse me," I pushed past her, heading for Tristam. I felt like any moment, this floor might drop out beneath me, but there was one thing I wanted to do before it did.

I reached his side and tapped him on the shoulder. He turned from the faerie he was talking with, and when he caught sight of me, his eyes opened ever so slightly in surprise. He hid it well, though, pasting on a sticky-sweet smile. "Jacq!" he said. "Congrats."

"I have something for you," I said, and then I reared back and punched him in the face.

Tristam reeled back into a crowd of faeries, clutching his cheek where I'd connected solidly. My hand throbbed like a sonuvabitch, and a flush of heat passed through me, as everything I had put my body through over the last few days caught up with me at once.

I tried to take a step back towards Patricia, who was hurrying our way with a delighted expression on her face, but my foot seemed like it was stuck in concrete.

"She punched me!" I heard Tristam's indignant howl as I toppled sideways, into Patricia's flimsy arms.

~

I CAME to in a hospital bed in a long, dark room. My head felt stuffed with wool, but my body was blissfully numb. They must have me on some sort of painkiller. Good stuff, too. I blinked to take in my surroundings and saw that the burn on my arm was bandaged.

There were beds around me filled with other contestants. It seemed everyone was asleep, it must be nighttime. Orin was in the bed next to me breathing evenly. When I saw his prone form, I sighed in relief. Then a spasm went through me. I was relieved to have him by my side. I was thinking, even in this moment, how he looked like a dark angel when he slept. I shoved the thought aside ruthlessly.

I realized then that someone had changed my clothes, and I was in a hospital gown. My jacket...it had the letter from Cass. I fumbled around the bed, looking underneath it. There. I let out a breath. Someone had piled my clothes neatly beneath the chair beside my bed. I stretched down to grab the letter when the door of the room clicked open. I pushed myself back up, my senses on alert.

The click of boots on the polished tiles of the floor was deafening amongst the soft breathing. When the figure came into view, I shook my head to be sure it wasn't a mirage. The Faerie king. Vale Obanstone himself.

He wore a pair of tan trousers and dark equestrian boots, together with a soft grey sweater. He looked like a British noble who just came in from a ride in the country. But his eyes were sharp, glowing slightly in the dark.

He stopped at my bed, and our eyes met. "You're awake," he said softly.

I nodded, swallowing. Just being alone with this man made me wish I had some sort of weapon. He was a predator. That was easy enough to see.

"Do you mind if I sit?" he nodded to the chair, and through I desperately wanted to say no, I nodded again. "It's your kingdom," I croaked.

He settled into the rickety wooden chair as if it was a throne. "You impressed me, Jacq," he said. "You and Orin both. No one expected you to make it to the first checkpoint. But you two have become a fan favorite."

"Everyone likes an underdog," I said weakly.

"Indeed. You're in last place starting the next trial, but you're still in it. I'm sure no one will underestimate you in the future."

Last place. His words were a gut punch. But he was right. We were still in it. We were better off than poor Gen and Zee, or even Yael and Duncan. We were still in it. I still had a chance to find Cass.

The king let out a little laugh and shook his head. "You Cunninghams do have spirit. I'll give you that."

He reached in the pocket of his sweater and drew something out. But I couldn't focus, because his words were like a maelstrom within me. *You Cunninghams*...like I wasn't the first Cunningham he had met. That he had known... A horrible thought overtook me, as the blood roared through my ears. Did the king have something to do with Cass's disappearance? Did he know where she was?

"Here," the king said, holding out the object. I looked at it. It was little glass vial on a chain with two pearls in it.

I shook my head woodenly. I wanted nothing from him. I wanted him gone. I wanted to bury my fingers in the wool of his sweater and pummel him until he told me what he knew about Cass. But I could only shake my head. "I don't want anything from the Obanstones," I managed.

He let out a rueful laugh. "I suppose we deserve that. Tristam's competitive side can sometimes...carry him away."

"He trapped us in a never-ending cave," I replied.

"Well, you ended up fine." The king waved away his son's transgressions, and my concerns, like a buzzing fly. "This isn't from me. It's part of the race. Everyone else got theirs at the ceremony, but you and Orin were in such bad shape, you missed it. You'll need it for the next trial."

I took the vial from him, and as my fingers brushed his, they burned. Yes, this man was dangerous. Just like his kingdom. Beautiful on the surface with deadly force lurking beneath.

28

The next morning dawned way too soon. It was barely light out when we were all unceremoniously pulled from our beds and thrust into a nearby room where the studio's make-up team had the unenviable job of making us look presentable.

Orin limped beside me, leaning on a black cane for support as we were each escorted to a chair.

"I'm surprised you can walk at all," I mumbled as the makeup artist began to pull out a mountain of bottles and brushes. "I thought for sure your ankle was broken."

"Shh," hissed Orin, nodding over to the other contestants. "Don't speak about the race. They'll be listening."

I looked over to the remaining contestants. Thankfully they'd put Tristam at the farthest chair away from me. He was happily chatting away to the young girl doing his hair, and as I watched, she let out a peal of laughter. Argh! I couldn't believe I'd actually liked the guy. Turning back to Orin I lowered my voice. "How is it? Your ankle?"

"I'm more concerned about the fact that I have to wear makeup," he fussed, throwing his makeup artist a dark look which made her cower. "It was broken. They've fixed it with magic. It's fine now."

"So why the cane?" I whispered.

Orin leaned close to my ear, causing his artist to huff. "You and I know I'm all right, but I don't want the others to know." He threw a glance at Molly who was on my other side. "Let them think we're weak. It could work in our favor. Besides, I think the cane makes me look distinguished."

I rolled my eyes, biting back a retort and looked at the room around me instead. As we'd just moved from one to the next, I guessed that we hadn't been in a hospital at all, rather a huge house. The Faerie king's country home? It looked ornate enough to be a palace. The cavernous space they'd stuck us in was big enough to be a ballroom; we only took up a corner of it. The tall director's-style chairs were filled with the remaining eight contestants.

I scoped our competition. Beside Molly sat her teammate Ario. I'd not seen much of them the whole race, they'd kept to themselves which in my opinion was the way to go. I had a feeling we should not underestimate them for the next round. I would still bet money that it was those two who lit a fire in the faerie hill when we were in the weird, creepy mirror world.

Next to Ario sat Phillip and Dulcina. Another pair that hadn't seen the limelight much, although they were, by far, the best-looking couple here. They wouldn't have looked out of place on the cover of a trendy magazine.

Finally, there was Sophia and Tristam. My blood boiled as I took in the pair of them lapping up the attention from their artists, so I decided to concentrate on my own reflection in the makeshift mirror they'd set up.

I looked haggard. Dark circles shadowed my eyes, and my skin looked washed out, giving me a ghostly look. If this was what a week over the Hedge did to a person, it was a miracle these faeries looked so damn beautiful all the time. Maybe it worked in opposites. What made faeries more gorgeous robbed humans of their vibrancy.

"I think you're going to need more make-up," I joked half-heartedly to my artist.

I closed my eyes as she worked away, not really caring about what I looked like. My thoughts were still firmly set on Cass and the fact that I was so close to her. If we *were* in the Faerie king's palace, that meant we were right in the heart of Elfame. If only I could just stand up and walk outside without anyone noticing.

"You're done!" My make-up artist trilled. Someone, a member of the palace staff or a studio lackey maybe, took me to another room, this one much smaller with a long rack of dresses and one very grumpy looking Orin.

"Now is your chance to shine," the thin brunette said, giving me a broad grin. "I'm your personal stylist, and I'm here to help you make the right choice for the interviews later. I've picked out a selection of dresses from the hottest human and fae designers. You want to make an impression, so I was thinking this one..." She pulled out a dress that looked like the sparkling night sky. It was covered in black shimmering sequins interspersed with silver ones like stars. It certainly was something special. I could imagine it on an Oscar winner, but I couldn't see me in it.

"I'm not wearing a dress. Bring me a clean outfit for the next trial."

The stylist's face dropped, and she looked at me as if I'd just asked to be dressed in a gown made of the finest artisanal dog poop.

Beside me, Orin nodded. "Yep, same for me."

"You know this is going to be broadcast throughout both

Earth and Faerwild. The others will be doing everything to get the attention of the audience," she protested.

"I suspect that if we go out in our race outfits while all the others are dolled up to the nines, we'll be the ones getting the attention, not that I care," I said.

The stylist tried everything she could think of to change our minds, but it was only when Orin picked up the sky dress and said he'd like to wear it himself, that she finally left the room to get us what we wanted.

In my mind, I could see John banging his head against his desk as he watched me walk onto the stage in my leggings and zip up FFR jacket, but I didn't care. I didn't join this race to be famous or popular, and I'd had enough pandering to everyone. I just wanted the interviews over so we could start the next part of the race. With any luck, it would be held in the city, making it easy for me to look into Cass's whereabouts without drawing too much attention.

"I'll come back and let you know when you're on," huffed the woman, clearly embarrassed by our style decision. "You two are on last. Hopefully, everyone will have turned their TVs off by that point." And with that, she stalked out, leaving us all alone.

"I think the black would have looked good on me," chuckled Orin as I took a seat next to him.

"You do have the ass for it," I agreed.

"You've been checking out my ass, have you?" Orin raised an eyebrow.

My face colored. "I was kidding. This whole thing is a pile of crap. Who cares what we wear?"

Orin raised his other eyebrow. "But what about the adoring fans?" he said in a simpering voice that was supposed to be Patricia.

I shook my head and laughed. "I know I should care, but

those millions of people watching don't mean anything when we're out in the field. They won't help us at all."

Orin placed his hand on my arm sending an unexpected shiver through me. "Have you ever thought your sister might be watching?"

No, the thought hadn't crossed my mind. But it was possible. What if she'd seen everything? Had Ben or any of the secret cameras placed strategically throughout the playing field managed to capture me reading Cass's letter? Would she have seen it and known to come find me? I threw the thought away. If she'd been watching, she'd have known where I was, and if that were the case, she'd have demanded to be let in to see me.

"Cass wouldn't care if I walked onto the stage naked."

Orin's choked back a cough. "Now that would get the ratings up!"

I playfully punched his arm and looked around. The room we were in was decorated so beautifully.

"Do you think we are at the Fae palace?" I asked.

"I think one of the smaller palaces. I'm not sure they would have transported us all the way to Elfame." Smaller palaces? Ugh. I knew Tristam, and his dad were pompous asses, but how many palaces does a ruler need?

The woman came back, the look of disgust still firmly set on her face. "Okay, you two are on. Come with me."

We followed her back into the main hall and then turned into what looked like the backstage of an auditorium. Past some curtains, I could see the stage and a wide bowl filled with rows of seating. And those seats were filled.

I stumbled at the sight.

"What's the matter?" Orin asked, stopping beside me.

The stylist continued walking, not even noticing.

"I didn't expect there to be people there."

"What did you expect?"

I shrugged my shoulders, trying not to let the fear in. "I thought it would just be us and Patricia. When everyone kept saying stage, I thought they meant a sound stage, not an actual one."

Orin took my hand, gripping it firmly. "We've been through worse together, I'm sure we'll get through this."

Taking a deep breath, I walked forward. As soon as the crowd saw us, they went wild, the noise filling the room, threatening to overwhelm me.

I plastered a fake smile on my face as Orin and I stepped out onto the stage.

Tristam and the others, having already been interviewed, were already sitting on two large sofas. Patricia greeted us, guiding us to the sofa. With dismay, I saw that the space left for us was next to Tristam. I tried to walk behind Orin so he'd end up sitting next to the traitor, but Patricia was having none of it.

She pulled Orin back, so I had to sit next to Tristam. When she was happy that we were all where she wanted us, she took a seat opposite.

"Good morning Jacqueline and Orin! It's nice to see you here and in such interesting outfit choices."

I glanced over at the other females. Molly was dressed in black as usual, but she looked stunning in a long velvet ballgown. Dulcina had picked a lilac dress to match her hair, and I noticed her make-up artist had liberally sprinkled her with sparkles. On the other side of Tristam sat Sophia who must have told her stylist to find her a dress that showed as much skin as possible. Her long tanned legs showed through a split in her dress right up to her panty line, and her cleavage defied gravity.

I'd made a huge mistake in coming out like this.

Sophia offered me a fake smile, and I had to stifle the urge to give her a matching black eye to Tristam's.

"We don't need to dress to impress," Orin began. "We're here to win a race, not a beauty pageant."

"As if they'd win one of those," I heard Sophia whisper not so subtly to Tristam.

"Of course," Patricia purred. "We've seen some of the highlights of the others' time in the race. Would you like to see some of yours?"

I had a feeling that saying "no" wasn't an option, so I nodded my head. A huge screen to the side of the stage came to life. I nearly died when I saw which moment they'd chosen to show. I closed my eyes as the onscreen me followed Tristam out of the cave.

I already knew what happened next. Tristam gave me the talisman and then kissed me slowly on the cheek. I thanked everything that was holy that we'd not kissed on the lips. I didn't think I'd have been able to bear the embarrassment. The crowd cheered, making me open my eyes at just the wrong moment. On the screen, because of the angle of the camera, it looked like we'd kissed on the lips. Beside me, I felt Orin go stiff.

Then his cheeks darkened as on the screen he woke up and placed the blanket over my sleeping form. So, it had been Orin, not Tristam as I had thought.

The screen flickered, and another shot unfolded. Tristam was now kissing Sophia behind a campfire. The whole thing made me gag. I'd been royally played, and now it was being shown for all to see. Mortification didn't cover how embarrassed I felt.

The screen went blank, and Patricia turned her attention back to us.

"What do you make of that Orin?"

"She was cold, I put a blanket on her," he answered simply, choosing not to elaborate. Patricia waited patiently for me to jump in and when it became apparent that I wasn't going to, she turned back to the screen.

I watched, cringing as Tristam's necklace transported us to that infernal cave followed by a scene of him and Sophia stealing two horses that Ario and Molly had somehow found. They really were both a sack of shit, but, at least, I wasn't the only one who had been fooled by Team Pretty Face.

At least, it wasn't them who'd tried to set us on fire when we were inside the enchanted mirror, burning all our supplies in the process. No, that was Phillip! Well, well. It seemed we could trust no one. I'd known from the start that we were on our own, and Orin had warned me time and time again, but I still found myself shocked at how outrageously awful the contestants had been to each other. Anger seethed within me as I took in all their misdeeds, making me more determined than ever to beat the lot of them. I was here to find Cass, but after everything I'd just witnessed, I needed something else too. I needed to win.

"Thank you all for coming out," boomed a voice as the large screen grew dark. The Faerie king strode onto the stage, his arms out wide in greeting towards the crowd.

"The first trial in the Fantastic Faerie Race is over, and we've seen plenty of action. Before I go on, we should have a moment's silence for our fallen contestants."

A montage of Genevieve and Zee brightened the screen, and throughout the auditorium, heads bowed. Anger bloomed within me at the thought of the Faerie king and Patricia feigning sorrow for the cameras. Like they hadn't been the ones behind their deaths.

As the king began speaking again, a flood of memories

came back to me, like missing pieces of a jigsaw puzzle. Niall and Patricia meeting secretly, Niall mentioning the Brotherhood, someone stealing the books from my room. Zee's ring not working. Something sinister was going on that went way beyond a race for TV, but what? Another memory flittered through my mind. The rose and thistle emblem on the boxes hidden in the dragon's lair—it was the same as the earrings Patricia had been wearing when we were all at Hennington House. And then, there was Cass and her indecipherable letter to Gen. Somehow she was involved in all of this, but for the life of me, I couldn't figure out how.

My mind was brought back to the present as the king raised his voice.

"And let's give a hand to all our remaining contestants. The next trial, the Elemental Trial, starts in two days."

Two days? My stomach dropped. That meant I had forty-eight hours to figure out what the hell was going on—or the next moment of silence might be for me.

IF YOU ENJOYED THE SORCERY TRIAL...

And now for a Sneak Peek of *The Elemental Trial*, Book Two in *The Faerie Race* trilogy!

You can buy the whole series now
The Sorcery Trial (Faerie Race book one)
The Elemental Trial (Faerie Race book two)
The Doomsday Trial (Faerie Race book three)

THE ELEMENTAL TRIAL CHAPTER ONE

I sat on the floor, holding a potted fern, talking to a magic bunny. No, the Fantastic Faerie

Race hadn't driven me completely insane. Though, there were still two more trials that could

claim that distinguished honor.

I closed my eyes again, blowing out a long breath. I had no idea what time it was; my

room in Hennington House didn't have a clock, and my phone was across the room. I thought

it was morning. In my mind's eye, I saw the etheric rabbit that represented my magic—my

power over the element of earth. In the past few hours of my pathetic efforts, the rabbit had

grown much more comfortable with me which seemed weird because it was all in my head.

Wasn't it?

The plant was nestled between my crossed legs. I was trying to move the dirt inside

the pot using my magic. I needed the bunny's help for that, which thus far, had not been forthcoming. Orin had told me that when he was a kid, he'd used magic by imagining the

different elements as pets. It had worked for me in the dragon's lair on Emerald Mountain at

the end of the last trial. I needed to be able to recreate it at will. Hence, plant. Hence, bunny.

"Come on," I coaxed. "Look at this wonderful dirt! So fragrant and full of nutrients. Don't

you want to move it? Let's move it together."

I knew I should be sleeping, but I'd given up on that after about three hours of tossing

and turning. My mind, assaulted by flashbacks of my days over the Hedge, refused to shut

down to allow me to get some much-needed rest. And I did need it. I wouldn't have the

luxury of a warm comforter or a soft mattress for long. The FFR had allowed us two nights

back in Wales to recuperate before we were to be thrown back into Faerwild and into the

second trial of the race.

It wasn't as though I wasn't tired—on the contrary, I was completely exhausted. But

every time I closed my eyes, I saw Zee's unblinking stare gazing up to the sky, or a swarm of

piranha-like Red Caps trying to eat Duncan and Yael alive. Being trapped in an endless

magic cave with no end in sight. Being chased by a panther. Being chased by an ancient tree-

like faerie king. Being chased—and caught—by a dragon. And then, there was Cass's letter.

If I was going to be honest with myself, it wasn't the danger of the next trial that had my mind whirring—it was the letter that Cass had written to Genevieve, and folded into the

shape of a flower just the way she used to send messages to me when we were little. A pang

of jealousy cut me as I thought of the note again. It meant she was alive—which was the part

I was concentrating on...but that knowledge brought another question. Why hadn't she tried

to contact me? Two years had passed without a word.

The bunny started to hop away as my mind wandered. "Wait!" I said to it, gesturing it

back. "I'm sorry. You're such a pretty bunny." It turned and hopped back towards me in my

mind, its little nose quivering. It was adorable. It sniffed my proffered hand, and then—to my

shock, it hopped into my arms. I let out a gasp of delight, stroking its soft fur. "Should we

move some dirt?" I swear its little nose quivered in affirmation. I focused on the plant,

pulling the power through the rabbit in my mind, and channeling it into the dirt. I just wanted

to raise it into the air slightly. I cracked one eye to peek and gasped as I saw that the dirt

around the fern's base was, in fact, floating ever so slightly.

A knock sounded on the door, and I yelped in surprise. The bunny leaped from my

mental arms, and dirt flew everywhere. I closed my eyes as it rained down on me. I sighed.

The knock sounded again. "Just a minute," I called. I opened my eyes, brushing dirt off my face and lashes. I had exploded the potted fern. "Great," I grumbled, standing and

shaking off the dirt and bits of plant as best I could.

I swung open the door and, to my surprise, found Ben standing there. I hadn't seen

him since we left Faerwild. All the camera people had traveled back to the human realm

separately from the contestants. Emotions welled in me, surprising me with their intensity.

Ben had been there for the hardest week of my life, and it was only now that we were both

out, both safe, that I realized just how much his presence had comforted me.

"Hi, Jacq," he said awkwardly as I flung myself into his arms.

"It's so good to see you."

He held me tightly and the stress I'd been feeling since we returned to Hennington

House melted away. Orin was my partner in the FFR, but Ben was my friend.

"Come in," I invited, untangling myself from him. "When did you get here?"

"We left Faerwild just before the contestants did, but the producers took us all out for

a meal and put us up for a night in a trendy hotel in Cardiff. Jacq..." he looked me up and

down, and surveyed the detritus in the room. "Did you know you're covered in dirt?"

"It's a long story." I brushed my face off again and pulled my hair from its ponytail,

doing my best to shake it out.

"I won't ask." He grinned.

"I think that's best."

"You all healed up? Ready for round two?"

"Hell, no," I said, shaking my head. "I haven't even been able to sleep. It's all

churning in my head. I keep remembering the endless cave and the Erl-king chasing us, and

just as I think I'm on the edge of sleep, the dragon pops into my head, and I'm wide awake

again."

Ben plopped himself on the bed, a serious expression on his face. "I'm sorry. I can

imagine. I was safe the whole time, thanks to all the protective enchantments they put on me,

but there were times I nearly shit myself out of fear. I'm not so sure you should go back in."

I looked across at him in surprise. "I've got to go back in. You know that."

"Why? Seriously, why do you have to go back in? There's no law that says you have

to. It's only a stupid TV show. Is it about the money? Because I'm not sure any amount of

money is worth risking your life for."

He spoke so earnestly I could feel myself being swayed. He had a point—Genevieve

and Zee had never made it back from Faerwild. But I wasn't doing it for the money. I was

doing it for something much more precious. The Faerie King's Boon. I needed to win to get

Cass back, and if I didn't win, I fully intended to stay in Faerwild until I found her. One way

or another, I was leaving the faerie realm with my sister.

Unfortunately, I couldn't articulate any of this to Ben. He didn't know about Cass, or at least, he didn't know more than the few bits he overheard when I was telling Orin. He

definitely didn't know that I had a letter from Cass hidden right under where he was sitting.

No one knew about it but me. Not even Orin.

"Think of everything I could do with a million dollars," I said, trying to sound

enthusiastic. "I'd never have to work again...or you know, living in L.A., I could buy a few

cups of coffee!"

Ben laughed at the joke before growing serious again. "I thought it would be fun, you

know, a bit of a laugh, a bit of danger...but it's not what I expected at all. They are paying

me really well, but..."

"But?" I raised my eyebrows.

"I knew I'd be safe in there, but I wasn't prepared for the emotional stress. There were

so many times I wanted to jump in and save you, but I knew that if I did, you'd be

disqualified and then you'd hate me forever."

"Are you thinking of quitting?" I asked. I tried to keep the panic from my voice at the

thought of being in there without him. Though we'd been able to say so little, he'd been a

comforting presence every step of the way.

Ben shook his head. "There's no way I'd let you go in there alone."

Relief flooded me. I scooted closer to him and hugged him again. "You're a good

friend, Ben. I'm glad you're my camera guy."

"Me too."

"Feel free to sneak me more protein bars at any time," I said, pushing to my feet.

Suddenly, I had realized how close we were, sitting side by side on the bed.

"Noted." He stood as well.

"Is that why you came to see me?" I asked. "Just to chat and tell me I'm a colossal

idiot if I go back over the Hedge?"

"Actually, no. And I don't think you're a colossal idiot. You're just braver than any

person has a right to be."

"That's what Orin said," I grumbled.

"The guy does know a few things," Ben said grudgingly. "But I came to get you.

There's a breakfast meeting in the dining hall in ten minutes."

Breakfast? I must have been working on my magic longer than I thought. I grabbed

my thin jacket from a chair where I'd thrown it, beckoned Ben, and together we headed out

the door, leaving the mess of dirt and fern behind.

The dining room was packed, leaving very little room to sit down. At the front of the

room stood Gabe, Evaline, and unfortunately, Patricia. She regarded me with a sickening

smile on her face as I searched the tables to find a place to sit. Ben had sat down near the

back with the other camera people.

I, on the other hand, would have to pick my way through the crowded room until I

found a seat. And then I saw him. Orin. My heart leapt as I saw he had an empty seat next to

him. As I made my way around the tables, I reflected on

how much things had changed since

I'd left Hennington House the first time. Before entering the race, I'd have sat literally

anywhere to avoid the empty space next to Orin. Now, I was glad that he'd saved me a seat.

Like it or not, Orin had become my only ally in the FFR, and he was the closest thing I had to

a friend. He gave me a smile as I eased myself into the chair beside him.

"Welcome, everyone, and to our contestants, welcome back," Gabe said, his arms

crossed and his feet spread as though he was about to send us into training. "I know you're all

hungry and waiting for your breakfast, so I'll keep this brief. I want to let you know how

proud I am of you all. I couldn't go into Faerwild, but you can bet I watched every second of

it on TV. You all worked so hard to come through, and I know you'll kill it in the next trial.

Of course, not everyone did get through. Yael and Duncan used their rings to get out as you

know. They are both back home with their families, and last I heard, they were negotiating

sponsorship deals with advertisers. That's what you can expect when you come back through.

You won't have seen the coverage, but the FFR is huge over here. Ratings have skyrocketed

and like it or not, you guys are famous the world over."

I swallowed hard at this news. Despite wanting to work in movies, fame had never

been a motivating factor. In fact, I'd like to remain as anonymous as possible. I guess that was a pipe dream. Looking around me, I saw that most of the other contestants were

practically salivating at the thought of it. When I glanced back at Orin, he grimaced. Maybe

we were more alike than I thought.

"Of course, Yael and Duncan aren't the only team we're missing today. You all know

what happened to Genevieve and Zee. It was a tragic accident and the..." I didn't hear the rest

of Gabe's sentence because rage filled my head, its dull roar drowning out his words. Yes,

Genevieve and Zee had died, but I was convinced it wasn't an accident at all. I wanted to

stand up and shout the truth to everyone—their rings had been disabled. They'd been robbed

of the chance to do what Duncan and Yael did and get out when they were in danger. There

would be no lucrative media contracts for Genevieve and Zee. They were gone.

It was only when I felt Orin's hand on my arm that I realized I was shaking.

"You okay?" he whispered, but I didn't reply. I wasn't sure I would be able to keep

my cool.

"You have one full day and night to yourselves before you go back into Faerwild for

the Elemental Trial, and I suggest you use it to rest. We haven't set a schedule for you

beyond mealtimes, but none of you are allowed to leave the grounds of Hennington House.

Tomorrow after breakfast, we need you all packed and ready to go back over the Hedge."

A chain of wait staff burdened with dishes were filing into the room, filling the air

with the smell of bacon and eggs. Gabe, knowing he couldn't compete with breakfast, gave

us a little bow and headed to a table in the corner along with Evaline and a number of FFR

staff.

I stood to join the line to get breakfast, but as I did, I noticed Patricia sneaking out of

the room. She looked like she was in a hurry. I hustled through the tables, battling the people

all going in the opposite direction to get breakfast. I needed to find out what she was up to. I

didn't have a shred of evidence that Patricia had anything to do with Gen and Zee's deaths,

but my gut told me something was off about that woman. The secret meetings with Niall, the

rose and thistle earrings she wore that just happened to be the same symbol as one I saw on

the box in the dragon's lair. I was determined to discover what she was hiding—and I had

only a day and night to do so.

Unfortunately, it took me so long to get through the crowd of hungry people that by

the time I got to the door, she was already gone.

THE ELEMENTAL TRIAL CHAPTER TWO

I ate until my stomach stretched, and then, I went back for thirds. Orin, on his second helping

of pancakes, raised an eyebrow at my plate covered in fluffy eggs, hash browns, and sausage.

"I'm never taking food for granted again," I said.

"We do need to stock up for another week of eating grass and tree bark," Orin said,

drowning his pancakes with syrup.

My phone buzzed in my jacket pocket, and my brow furrowed. It was the third time

since I'd come down to breakfast.

"You going to get that?" Orin asked.

"I'm avoiding them."

"Who's them?"

"My parents," I said around a bite of sausage.

"Have you talked to them since you've been back?"

I shook my head. I couldn't bring myself to face them. I knew I needed to tell them

about Cass, but I didn't know exactly what there was to tell. Hey Mom, Dad, I think your

long-lost daughter is alive and neck-deep in some mysterious faerie conspiracy... it sounded
crazy.

"I know it's none of my business." A pained look flashed
across Orin's handsome
face. "But...if I could talk to my parents, I definitely
wouldn't miss the chance."

I recoiled. "You can't even talk to them?"

He shook his head, looking over his shoulder at Tristam
before leaning in. "The king
doesn't allow anyone into his palace without a royal invi-
tation. And they're not allowed out."

I glared at Tristam, who at that moment was a fine
stand-in for the king. "Dicks." I
sighed and pushed to my feet. Orin was right. And
besides, I didn't think I could physically
fit the food on my plate into my body. I'd overestimated.
"I'll go call them."

"Good girl," Orin said.

I grabbed my mug of coffee and walked into the hallway.
A cameraperson was
standing in the corner, stationed to catch any of us
coming out of the dining room. I cut to the
left, into the study where Niall once slurred his secrets to
me. Not that they had made any
sense. Ario and Molly were stationed in the two tall
chairs by the fire, leaning in to talk in
hushed tones. They turned to look at me as I entered,
and I held up my hands.

"Occupied," Molly said, sickly sweetly. I noticed her
bubble gum pink hair had
changed to bright blue. When she'd had time to re-dye

it, I had no idea. My hair definitely

wasn't my top priority right now.

"Sorry." I turned on my heel and pushed deeper into the house, searching for a corner

away from prying eyes or blinking red lights. Finally, I found a little pantry, filled with

shelves heavy-laden with potatoes and jars of pickles and peaches. I sagged against the dusty

shelves, wiggling my nose to fight the tickle that threatened a sneeze.

I hit the callback button and tried to calm my nerves.

"Jacq!" My mother answered on the first ring. At the sound of her voice, a lump grew

in my throat.

"Hi, Mom," I managed, sagging down a shelf to the cold floor.

"Rick, it's Jacqueline! Get over here. We're going to put you on speaker, honey,

okay?"

"Okay," I said, trying to get a hold of the emotions threatening to crash over me. The

weight of the last week—the strain of hunger and cold and lack of sleep, of danger and death.

Of running for my life. Maybe this was the real reason I hadn't called. Because some part of

me had known that with them, I'd have to be real. They could spot my false bravado and

determination from a mile away. And beneath that, I was tired, and sad, and scared to go back

over the Hedge. I couldn't let myself feel those things.

I cleared my throat and cradled the phone against my shoulder, pressing the heels of

my hands to my eyes to hold in the tears.

"Jacq!" my father's voice. "My god, honey, you were magnificent out there!"

"Really?" I asked, looking up. That's not what I was expecting.

"Are you kidding? We're so proud of you!"

"I guess I did kill that panther," I said, a little smile creeping onto my face. "That

musta looked pretty cool."

"The panther, what about the dragon!" my dad boomed. "Doing Montana proud!"

At the mention of Montana, my smile dimmed. "How's everyone doing about

Genevieve?" Genevieve, the other contestant who had died, was from my same small town.

"The town's in mourning, the tribe especially. How tragic," my mom said. "I know

it's selfish to say, but I'm just glad you're safe."

"Me too," I said.

Mom continued. "Dad's proud of all your stunts, but I'm proud of your character,

sweetie. You saved Genevieve and her partner in that horrible faerie's house, and you were

going to save those idiots who blundered into the Red Cap nest. You never sacrificed your

values to get ahead. Hold fast to that in this next leg. Don't let it go."

"And stay away from that blond-haired jackass," Dad added. "He's trying to wrap you

around his finger. Don't let him play you. Us Cunninghams know better."

I let out a choked laugh. "Trust me, Dad, I learned that one the hard way. I won't make that mistake again." At the mention of Cunning-hams, I knew I needed to ask about

Cass. I wasn't ready to tell them what I'd found. Not until I knew more. But maybe they

could help.

"Hey, guys, can I ask you something?"

"Of course," they chimed together. God, I missed them. I missed home and the

scratchy blanket on the leather couch in front of the fire-place, and my mom's chocolate chip

cookies, and the smell of newsprint and coffee in the kitchen in the morning. Why had I not

been home to visit lately?

"Remember that old book they found in Cass's room? The leather one with the

symbol on the cover? That the ICCF took?"

Silence. "Yes," my mother finally said, the cheer drained from her voice. "Why do

you ask?"

"Being here...it's just bringing up a lot of stuff. I thought I saw the same book. I just

wanted to know."

"It was called A Disunion of Worlds," Dad said. "Not that they'd let us even get a

glimpse at it, the bastards. I've never been able to find a copy. Maybe you can find it over

there."

"Thanks. I'll take a look."

"I don't want you to get your hopes up, sweetie," Mom said, ever the practical one.

"We did a lot of searching after she was gone." She hesitated. "We didn't want to get ahead

of ourselves, so we didn't tell you about much. But...the

trail was cold, honey. I don't think

we'll ever see Cassandra again."

I had resigned myself to the same fate, but it still hurt to hear it coming from them.

Parents aren't ever supposed to give up on their child, are they? But I understood. They had

to find some way to live on.

Dad's voice went gruff. "Now you be careful out there. Play smart. Stick with Orin, it

seems like you two have a good partnership going. Keep your head in the game. We're not

going to let those faerie bastards take another daughter from us."

"Oh, Rick," my mom chided softly.

"They won't. I'll be careful. I plan to win this thing." I felt my resolve hardening

within me, my doubts and exhaustion draining away. I wouldn't tell them about my hopes, or

the boon—not until I had Cass back. The two of us would come walking up the driveway,

and it would be the four of us again. I would bring her back to them. If it was the last damn

thing I did.

"If anyone can do it, you can," Mom said.

"That means a lot," I said. "All right, I gotta go. I plan on eating and sleeping as much

as I can before we go back in there."

We said our goodbyes, and I hit the red button, cradling my phone to my chest. I had

been dreading calling my parents, worrying it would drain my energy and fill me with guilt.

Instead, it had buoyed me—given me new purpose. I would do this. I would go in there, kick some faerie ass, and win this thing.

I pushed to my feet, brushing the dust from my leggings. I opened the door, emerging

from the pantry into the dark hallway. I shut the door quietly and started heading back when I

heard a floorboard squeak behind me.

That was when someone threw a black hood over my head.

ABOUT J.A. ARMITAGE

J.A lives in a total fantasy world (because reality is boring right?) When she's not writing all the crazy fun in her head, she can be found eating cake, designing pretty pictures and hanging upside down from the tallest climbing frame in the local playground while her children look on in embarrassment. She's travelled the world working as everything from a banana picker in Australia to a Pantomime clown, has climbed to the top of Mount Kilimanjaro and the bottom of the Grand Canyon and once gave birth to a surrogate baby for a friend of hers.

She spends way too much time gossiping on Facebook and if you want to be part of her Reading Army, where you'll get lots of freebies, exclusive sneak peeks and super secret sales, join up here https://www.subscribepage.com/v7o8l

ABOUT CLAIRE LUANA

Claire Luana grew up in Seattle reading everything she could get her hands on and writing every chance she could. Eventually, adulthood won out, and she turned her writing talents to more scholarly pursuits, going to work as a commercial litigation attorney.

While continuing to practice law, Claire decided to return to her roots and try her hand once again at creative writing. She has written and published the four fantasy series: the Moonburner Cycle, the Confectioner Chronicles, the Knights of Caerleon, co-written with Jesikah Sundin, and The Faerie Race, co-written with J.A. Armitage.

She lives in Seattle, Washington with her husband and two dogs. In her (little) remaining spare time, she loves to hike, travel, binge-watch CW shows, and of course, fall into a good book.

Connect with Claire Luana online at:

Website & Blog: http://www.claireluana.com
Facebook: http://www.facebook.com/claireluana
Twitter: http://www.twitter.com/clairedeluana
Goodreads: https://www.goodreads.com/author/show/15207082.Claire_Luana
Instagram: http://www.instagram.com/claireluana

ALSO BY J.A. ARMITAGE

Reverse Fairytales

Charm

Lucky Charm

Charmed

Dark Water

Blue Water

Breakwater

Dragon Slayer

Slayer

Warrior

Protector

The Faerie Race

The Sorcery Trial

The Elemental Trial

The Doomsday Trial

ALSO BY CLAIRE LUANA

Moonburner Cycle

Moonburner, Book One

Sunburner, Book Two

Starburner, Book Three

Burning Fate, Prequel Novella

Confectioner Chronicles

The Confectioner's Guild, Book One

The Confectioner's Coup, Book Two

The Confectioner's Truth, Book Three

The Confectioner's Exile, Prequel Novella

The Knights of Caerleon, with Jesikah Sundin

The Fifth Knight, Book One

The Third Curse, Book Two

The First Gwenevere, Book Three

Orion's Kiss

The Faerie Race

The Sorcery Trial (Faerie Race book one)

The Elemental Trial (Faerie Race book two)

The Doomsday Trial (Faerie Race book three)